## HARLEQUIN®
### *Presents*

Welcome to the January 2009 collection of Harlequin Presents!

This month be sure to catch the second installment of Lynne Graham's trilogy VIRGIN BRIDES, ARROGANT HUSBANDS with her new book, *The Ruthless Magnate's Virgin Mistress.* Jessica goes from office cleaner to the billionaire boss's mistress in Sharon Kendrick's *Bought for the Sicilian Billionaire's Bed,* and sexual attraction simmers uncontrollably when Tara has to face the ruthless count in *Count Maxime's Virgin* by Susan Stephens. You'll be whisked off to the Mediterranean in Michelle Reid's *The Greek's Forced Bride,* and in Jennie Lucas's *Italian Prince, Wedlocked Wife,* innocent Lucy tries to resist the seductive ways of Prince Maximo. A ruthless tycoon will stop at nothing to bed his convenient wife in Anne McAllister's *Antonides' Forbidden Wife,* and friends become lovers when playboy Alex Richardson needs a bride in Kate Hardy's *Hotly Bedded, Conveniently Wedded.* Plus, in Trish Wylie's *Claimed by the Rogue Billionaire,* attraction reaches the boiling point between Gabe and Ash, but can either of them forget the past?

We'd love to hear what you think about Presents. E-mail us at Presents@hmb.co.uk or join in the discussions at www.iheartpresents.com and www.sensationalromance.blogspot.com, where you'll also find more information about books and authors!

Bedded by... *Blackmail*

Forced to bed...then to wed?

He's got her firmly in his sights and she's got only one chance of survival—surrender to his blackmail...and him...in his bed!

**Bedded by... Blackmail**

**The *big* miniseries from Harlequin Presents®**

**Dare you read it?**

# Michelle Reid

## THE GREEK'S FORCED BRIDE

Bedded by...  Blackmail

Forced to bed...then to wed?

# HARLEQUIN®

TORONTO • NEW YORK • LONDON
AMSTERDAM • PARIS • SYDNEY • HAMBURG
STOCKHOLM • ATHENS • TOKYO • MILAN • MADRID
PRAGUE • WARSAW • BUDAPEST • AUCKLAND

ISBN-13: 978-0-373-12788-7
ISBN-10:     0-373-12788-X

THE GREEK'S FORCED BRIDE

First North American Publication 2009.

Copyright © 2008 by Michelle Reid.

www.eHarlequin.com

Printed in U.S.A.

All about the author...
*Michelle Reid*

Reading has been an important part of
**MICHELLE REID**'s life since as far back as she
can remember. She was encouraged by her mother,
who made the twice-weekly bus trip to the nearest
library to keep feeding this particular hunger in all
five of her children. In fact, one of Michelle's most
abiding memories from those days is coming home
from school to find a newly borrowed selection of
books stacked on the kitchen table just waiting to
be delved into.

There has not been a day since that she hasn't
had at least two books lying open somewhere in
the house, ready for her to pick up and continue
whenever she has a quiet moment.

Her love of romance fiction has always been
strong, though she feels she was quite late in
discovering the riches Harlequin novels have to
offer. It wasn't long after making this discovery
that she made the daring decision to try her
hand at writing a Presents book for herself, never
expecting it to become such an important part of
her life.

Now she shares her time between her large,
close, lively family and writing. She lives
with her husband in a tiny white-stoned cottage
in the English Lake District. It is both a romantic
haven and the perfect base from which to go
walking through some of the most beautiful
scenery in England.

# CHAPTER ONE

LOUNGING in his chair at the head of the boardroom table, Leo Christakis, thirty-four-year old human dynamo and absolute head of the Christakis business empire, held the room in a state of near-rigid tension by the sheer power of his silence.

No one dared to move. All dossiers resting on the long polished table top remained firmly closed. Except for the folder flung open in front of Leo. And as five minutes edged with agonising slowness towards ten, even the act of breathing in and out became a difficult exercise and not one of those present had the nerve to utter so much as a sound.

For Leo's outwardly relaxed posture was dangerously deceptive, as was the gentle way he was tapping his neatly clipped fingernails on the polished surface as he continued to read. And anyone—anyone daring to think that the sensual shape of his mouth was relaxed in a smile needed a quick lesson in the difference between a smile and a sneer.

Leo knew the damn difference. He also knew that the nasty stuff was about to hit the fan. For someone around here had pulled a fast one with company money and what made him really angry was that the fiddle was so badly put together anyone with a rudimentary grasp of arithmetic could spot it a mile away. Leo did not employ incompetents. Therefore the list of employees who might just dare to believe they could get away with ripping him off like this could be shortlisted to one.

Rico, his vain and shallow, gut-selfish stepbrother, and the only person employed by this company to earn his place in it by favour alone.

Family, in other words.

Damn, Leo cursed within the depths of his own angry thinking. What the hell gave Rico the idea he could get away with this? It was well known throughout this global organisation that each branch was hit regularly by random internal audits for the specific purpose of deterring anyone from trying a stunt like this. It was the only way a multinational the size of this one could hope to maintain control!

The arrogant fool. Was it not enough that he was paid a handsome salary for doing almost nothing around here? Where did he get off believing he could dip his greedy fingers in the pot for more?

'Where is he?' Leo demanded, bringing half a dozen heads shooting up at the sudden sound of his voice.

'In his office,' Juno, his London based PA quickly responded. 'He was informed about this meeting, Leo,' the younger man added in case Leo was living with the mistaken belief that Rico had not been told to attend.

Leo did not doubt it, just as he did not doubt that everyone sitting around this table believed that Rico was about to receive his just desserts. His stepbrother was a freeloader. It went without saying that the people who worked hard for their living did not like freeloaders. And all it took was for him to lift his dark head with its hard, chiselled bone structure, which would have been stunningly perfect if it weren't for the bump in the middle of his slender nose—put there by a football boot when he was in his teens—and scan with his rich, dark velvet brown eyes half a dozen carefully guarded expressions to have that last thought confirmed.

*Theos.* There was little hope of him managing to pull off a cover-up with so many people in the know and silently baying for Rico's blood, he concluded as he hid his eyes again beneath the thick curl of his eyelashes.

Did he *want* to cover up for Rico? The question flicked at the muscle that lined his defined jawbone because Leo knew the answer was yes, he did prefer to affect a cover-up than to deal with the alternative.

A thief in the family.

Fresh anger surged. With it came a grim flick of one hand to shut the folder before he rose to his feet, long legs thrusting him up to his full and intimidating six feet four inches immaculately encased in a smooth dark pinstripe suit.

Juno also jumped up. 'I will go and—'

'No, you will not,' Leo said in tightly accented English. 'I will go and get him myself.'

Everyone else shifted tensely as Juno sank down in his seat again. If Leo had been in the mood to notice, he would have seen the wave of swift, telling glances that shifted around the table, but he was in no frame of mind to want to notice anything else as he stepped around his chair and strode out through the door without bothering to spare anyone another glance.

Just as he didn't bother to look sideways as he strode across the plush hushed executive foyer belonging to the Christakis London offices. If he had happened to glance to the side, then he would have seen the lift doors were about to open—but he didn't.

He was too busy cursing the sudden heart attack that took his beloved father from him two years ago, leaving him with the miserable task of babysitting the two most irritating people it had been his misfortune to know—his high-strung Italian stepmother, Angelina, and her precious son, Rico Giannetti.

*Ah, someone save me from smooth, handsome playboys and hypersensitive stepmothers anxiously besotted with their beautiful sons*, he thought heavily. Family loyalty was the pits, and the day that Rico's ever-looming marriage took place and he took his life and his gullible new wife back to his native Milan to live with Angelina, could not come soon enough for Leo.

*If* he could get Rico out of this mess without compromising his own reputation and standing in this company that was, or Rico would not be going anywhere but a prison cell.

A sigh hurt his chest as Leo chose to suppress it, the knowledge that he was already looking for a way out for Rico scraping the sides of his pride in contempt.

What was Natasha going to do if she found out she was about to marry a thief?

Though why the hell his stepbrother had chosen to marry Miss Cool and Prim Natasha Moyles was a mystery to Leo. She was not the nubile celebrity stick-like variety of female Rico usually turned on for. In fact, she lived inside a pretty much perfect long-legged and curvy hourglass shape she ruined by hiding it with her lousy dress sense. She was also cold and polite and irritatingly standoffish—around Leo anyway.

So why Natasha had fallen in love with a life-wasting playboy like Rico was just another puzzle Leo could not work out. The attraction of opposites? Did the cool and prim disguise fall apart around Rico?

Perhaps she became a bodice-ripping sex goddess in the bedroom, because she sure had the potential to be a raging sex goddess with her soft feminine features and her wide-spaced, too-blue eyes and that lush, sexy mouth she could not disguise, which just begged to be kissed out of its—

*Theos*, Leo cursed yet again as something familiarly hot gave a tug low down in his gut to remind how Natasha Moyles's mouth could affect him—while behind him the object of his thoughts walked out of the lift only to pull to a shuddering halt when she caught sight of his instantly recognisable, tall, dark suited shape striding into the corridor across the other side of the foyer.

Natasha's heart did a funny little squirm in her chest and for a moment she actually considered giving in to the sudden urge to leap back into the lift and come back to see Rico later when his stepbrother wasn't about.

She did not like Leo Christakis. He had an uncomfortable way of always making her feel tense and edgy with his hard-nosed, worldly arrogance and his soft, smooth sarcasms that always managed to make such accurate swipes at just about every insecurity she possessed.

Did he think she never noticed the sardonic little smile he always wore on his mouth whenever he was given an opportunity to run his eyes over her? Did he think it was great fun to make her freeze with agonising self-consciousness because she knew he was mocking the way she preferred to hide her curves rather than put them on show like the other women that circled his wonderful self?

Not that it mattered what Leo Christakis thought about her, Natasha then told herself quickly, while refusing to acknowledge the way her eyes continued to cling to him, or that one of her hands was nervously slotting a loose golden strand of hair back to her neatly pinned knot and the other hand clutched her little black purse to the front of her pale blue suit as if the purse acted like a piece of body armour meant to keep him at bay.

She wasn't here to see him. He was just the arrogant, self-important, overbearing stepbrother of the man she was supposed to be marrying in six weeks. And unless Rico had some very good answers to the accusations she was about to fire at him, then there wasn't going to be a wedding!

Natasha felt herself go pale as she recalled the scene some kind person had relayed to her mobile phone this morning. Why did some people take pleasure in sending another person images of their fiancé locked in the arms of another woman? Did they think that because she was attached to the pop-music industry she couldn't possibly have feelings to wound?

*Well, look at me now*, Natasha thought bleakly as she dragged her eyes away from Leo to stare at the way her trembling fingers were gripping her purse. *I'm not just wounded, I'm dying!* Or her love for Rico was dying, she revised bleakly. Because this was it, the final straw, the last time she was going to turn blind eyes and deaf ears to the rumours about his cheating on her.

It was time for a showdown.

Pale lips pressed together now, eyes fixed on the expanse of grey carpet spread out in front of her, Natasha set herself walking across the foyer and into the corridor that led the way to Rico's office in the now-forgotten wake of Leo Christakis.

The door was shut tight into its housing. Leo didn't bother to knock on it before he twisted the handles and threw it open wide, then took a long step forwards, ready to give Rico Giannetti hell—only to find himself freezing at the sight that met his flashing dark gaze.

For the next few numbing seconds Leo actually found himself wondering if he was dreaming what he was seeing. It was so difficult to believe that even Rico could be this crass! For standing there in front of his desk was his handsome stepbrother with his trousers pooled round his ankles and a pair of slender female legs wrapped around his waist. The very air in the room seethed with gasps as Rico's tight and tanned backside thrust forwards and backwards while soft groans emitted from the naked and not-so-prim female spread out on the top of the desk.

Clothes were scattered all over the place. The smell of sex was strong and thick. The very floor beneath Leo's feet vibrated to Rico's urgent gyrations.

'What the *hell*—?' Leo raked out in a blistering explosion of grinding disgust at the precise moment that an entirely separate sound hit him from behind and had him wheeling about.

He found himself staring into the shock-frozen face of Rico's fiancée. Confusion locked onto his hard golden features because he had believed the blonde ranging about on the desk must be her!

'Natasha?' he ground out in a surprise-driven rasp.

But Natasha didn't hear him. She was too busy seeing her worst nightmare confirmed by the two people who were beginning to realise they were no longer alone. As she watched as if from a strange place somewhere way off in the distance she saw Rico's handsome dark head lift up and turn. Sickness clawed at the walls of her stomach as his heavy-lidded, passion-glazed eyes connected with hers.

Then the woman moved, dragging Natasha's gaze sideways as a blonde head with a pair of blue eyes lifted up to peer around Rico's blocking frame. The two women looked at each other—that was all—just looked.

'*Who* the—?' Leo spun back the other way to discover that the two lovers were now aware of their presence.

The woman was trying to untangle herself, levering herself up on an elbow as she pushed at Rico's bared chest with a slender hand. Shifting his eyes to her, Leo felt true hell arrive as the full horror of what they were witnessing slammed like a truck into his face.

Cindy, Natasha's sister. Two blondes with blue eyes and an age gap that made Cindy seem still just a kid.

His stomach revolted. He swung back to Natasha, but Natasha was no longer standing behind him. Her tense long-legged curvy shape in its stiff pale blue suit was already half-way back down the corridor, making as fast as she could for the lift.

Anger on her behalf roaring up inside him, Leo twisted back to the two guilty lovers. The serious questions Rico should be answering suddenly flew right out of his head. 'You are finished with me, Rico,' he raked out at the younger man. 'Get your clothes on and get the hell out of my building before I have you thrown out—and take the slut with you!'

Then he walked out, pulling the door shut behind him before taking off after Natasha at a run and feeling an odd sense of disorientating empowerment now that Rico had given him just cause to kick him right out of his life.

The lift doors closed before he got there. Cursing through his clenched teeth, Leo turned and headed for the stairs. One flight down and the single lift up to the top floor became three lifts, which fed the whole building. Glancing up to note that Natasha was going down to the basement just before he strode inside another lift, he hit the button that would take him to the same place.

His insides were shaking. All of him was pumped up and pulsing because—*Theos*, sex did that to you. Even when what you'd seen sickened and disgusted, it still had a nasty way of playing its song in your blood.

Striding out of the lift, Leo paused to look around the basement car park. Natasha's Mini stood out like a shiny red stain in a murky world of fashionable silver and black. He saw her then. She was leaning heavily on the car and her shoulders were heaving. He thought she was weeping but as he approached her he realised that she was being violently sick.

'It's OK…' he muttered for some stupid reason because

nothing could be less *OK*, and he placed his hands on her shoulders.

'Don't touch me!' She jerked away from him.

Offence hit Leo full on his chiselled chin. 'I am not Rico!' he raked back in sheer reaction. 'Just as you are not your slut of a sister—!'

She turned and slapped him hard on the face.

The stinging slap rang around the basement as Leo rocked back on his heels in surprise. Natasha was quivering all over, nothing going on inside her burning brain but the remains of that searing surge of violence that had made her turn and lash out. She had never done anything like it before, not in her entire life!

Then she was suddenly having to reel away and double up to retch again, while sobbing and shaking and clutching at the car's bodywork with fingernails that scraped the shiny red paint.

Rico with Cindy—how could he?

How could *she*?

A pair of long fingered hands dared to take hold of her shoulders again. She didn't pull away, but just sagged like a quivering sack into his grasp as the final dregs of her stomach contents landed only inches away from her low heeled black shoes. By the time it was over she could barely stand upright.

Grim lips pressed together, Leo continued to hold her while she found a tissue in her jacket pocket and used it to wipe her mouth. Beneath the grip of his fingers he could feel her trembling. Her head was bowed, exposing the long, slender whiteness of her nape. That hot sensation flicked at his insides again and he looked away from her, flashing an angry look around the car park like a man being hunted by an invisible quarry and wondering what the hell he was going to do next.

She was not his problem, one part of his brain tried telling him. He had a meeting to chair and a serious financial discrepancy to deal with, plus a dozen or so other points of business to get through before he flew back to Athens this evening and...

A man suddenly appeared from the lurking shadows where the security offices were situated in a corner of the basement. It was Rasmus, his security chief, eyeing them curiously. Leo dismissed him with a frowning shake of his dark head that sent the other man melting back into the shadows again.

His next thought was to coax Natasha back into the lift and take her up to his own office suite to recover. But he could not guarantee that he could get her in there without someone—Rico or her sister—seeing them and starting up another ugly scene.

'OK now?' he dared to question once her trembling started to ease a little.

She managed a single nod. 'Yes. Thank you,' she whispered.

'This is not a moment for polite manners, Natasha,' he responded impatiently.

Natasha jerked away from him, hating him like poison for being here and witnessing her complete downfall like this. Receiving picture evidence that Rico was cheating on her was one thing, but to actually see him doing it with her own sister was absolutely something else.

Just thinking about it had fresh nausea trying to take a grip on her stomach. Working desperately to control it, Natasha fumbled in her bag for her car keys, then turned to unlock the Mini so she could reach inside it for the bottle of water she always kept in there. She wanted to dive into the car and just drive away from it all, but she knew she didn't have it in her yet to drive herself anywhere. She was still too shaken up, too sick and dizzy with horror and shock.

As she straightened up again she had to step around the mess she had ejected onto the ground. *He* didn't move a single inch so she brushed against him in an effort to gain herself some space. It was like brushing against barbed wire, she likened as a hot-rod prickle scraped down through her body and forced her to wilt backwards with a tremor of flayed senses against the side of the car.

Keeping her eyes lowered and away from Leo, she twisted the cap off the bottle of water and put it to her unsteady lips so she could take a couple of careful sips. Her heart was pounding in her head and her throat felt so thick it struggled to swallow. And he continued to stand there like some looming dark shadow, killing her ability to think and making her feel the insignificance of her own diminutive five feet six inches next to his overpowering height.

But that was the great and gloriously important Leo Christakis, she mused dismally—a big, tough, overpowering entity with a repertoire in sardonic looks and blunt comments that could shrivel a lesser person to pulp, and a brain that functioned for only one thing—making money. Even as she stood here refusing to look at him she could feel him fighting the urge to glance at his watch, because he must have more important things to do with his time than to stand here wasting it on her.

'I'll be all r-right in a minute,' she managed. 'You can go back to work now.'

She'd said that as if she believed work was the only thing he lived for, Leo picked up. His chiselled chin jutted. Natasha Moyles always had a unique way of antagonising him with her polite, withdrawn manner or her swift, cool glances that dismissed him as if he were nothing worthy of her regard. She'd been doing it to him from the first time they were introduced at his stepbrother's London apartment.

Leo thrust his clenched hands into his trouser pockets, pushing back the flaps of his dark pinstripe jacket to reveal the pristine white front to his handmade shirt. She shifted jerkily as if the action threatened her somehow and he was suddenly made acutely aware of his own long, muscled torso and taut, bronzed skin. Even the layer of hair that covered his chest prickled.

'Take some more sips at the water and stop trying to out-guess what I might be thinking,' he advised coolly, not liking these sensations that kept on attacking him.

'I wasn't trying to—'

'You were,' he interrupted, adding curtly, 'You might dislike me intensely, Natasha, but allow me a bit more sensitivity than to desert you here after what you have just witnessed.'

But he did not possess quite enough sensitivity to hold back from reminding her of it! Natasha noted as the whole sickening horror of what she had seen sucked her right back in. Her inner world began to sway dizzily, the groan she must have uttered bringing his fingers back up to clasp her arms. She wanted to shrug him off, but she found that she couldn't. She needed his support because she had a horrible feeling that without it she was going to sink into a great dark hole in the ground.

An eerie-sounding beep suddenly echoed through the car park. It was the executive lift being called back up the building to pick up new passengers. Leo bit out a curse at the same time that Natasha's head shot up to stare at him, her wide, blue eyes clashing full on with his dark brown eyes. For a long moment neither of them moved as they stood trapped by a strange kind of energy that shimmered its way through Natasha's body right down to her toes.

*Theos*, she's beautiful, Leo heard himself think.

She made a sudden dive towards her open car door. Moving like lightning, Leo managed to get there before her, one set of fingers closing around her slender wrist to hold her back while he closed the car door, then took the keys from her hand.

'W-what—?'

Her stammered half-question was cut short by a man used

to making snap decisions. Leo turned and all but frogmarched her across the basement to where his own low sleek black car was parked.

'I can drive myself!' she protested when she realised what he was doing.

'No, you cannot.'

'But—'

'That could be Rico about to walk out of the lift,' he turned on her forcefully. 'So make your mind up, Natasha, which one of us would you prefer to be with right now!'

So very brutal in its delivery. Natasha's mind flooded yet again with what she had witnessed upstairs and she turned into a block of ice.

Opening the car door, Leo propelled her inside. She went without protest, accidentally dropping the water bottle as she did. Jaw set like a vice now, Leo closed the door as, like a man born with special mental powers, Rasmus reappeared not far away. Leo tossed her keys at him and didn't need to issue instructions. His security chief just slunk away again, knowing exactly what was expected of him.

Ignoring the fallen water bottle, Leo strode around the car and got in behind the wheel. She was huddled in the passenger seat, staring down at her two hands where they knotted together on the top of her little black purse and she was shivering like crazy now as the classic reaction to shock well and truly set in.

Pinning his lips together, Leo switched on the engine and thrust it into gear, then sent the car flying towards the exit on an ear-shattering screech of tires. They hit daylight and the early afternoon traffic in a seething atmosphere of emotional stress. A minute later his in-car telephone system burst into life, the screen on his dashboard flashing up Rico's name. A choice phrase locked in the back of his throat and he flicked a switch on the steering wheel that shut the phone down.

Ten seconds later and Natasha's phone started to ring inside her bag.

'Ignore it,' he gritted.

*'Do you think I am stupid?'* she choked out.

Then they both sat there in thick, throbbing silence, listening to her phone ring until her voicemail took over the call. Her phone kept on ringing repeatedly as they travelled across London with the two of them sitting there like waxwork dummies waiting for her voicemail to keep doing its thing while anger pumped adrenalin into Leo's bloodstream making his fingers grip the steering wheel too tight.

Neither spoke a word to each other. He didn't know what to say if it did not include a string of obscenities that would probably make this woman blanch.

Natasha, on the other hand, had closed herself off inside a cold little world filled with reruns of what she had witnessed. She knew that her sister's behaviour was out of control, but she'd never thought Cindy would sink so low as to...

She had to swallow to stop the bile from rising again as she replayed the moment when Cindy had seen her standing in the door. She saw the look of triumph hit her sister's face followed by the oh-so-familiar pout of defiance that revealed the truth as to why she was doing that with Rico.

Cindy didn't really want him. She did not even like him that much, but she could not stand the thought that Natasha had anything she hadn't first tried out for herself.

Selfish to the last drop of blood, Natasha thought painfully. Spoiled by two parents who liked to believe their youngest daughter was the most gifted creature living on this earth. She was prettier than Natasha, more outward-going than Natasha. Funnier and livelier and so much more talented than Natasha ever could or wanted to be.

Blessed, their parents called it, because Cindy could sing

like a bird and she was the latest pop discovery promising to set the UK alight. After a short stint on a national TV singing competition, Cindy's was the face that everyone recognised while Natasha stood in the background like a shadow. The quiet one, the invisible one whose job it was to make sure everything ran smoothly in her talented sister's wonderful life.

Why had she allowed it to happen? she asked herself now when it all felt so ugly. Why had she agreed to put her own life on hold and be drawn into playing babysitter to a self-seeking, spoiled brat who'd always resented having an older sister to share anything with?

Because she'd known their ageing parents couldn't cope with Cindy. Because from the moment that Cindy's singing talents had been discovered she'd realised that someone had to attempt to keep her from going right off the egotistic rails.

*And, face it, Natasha. At first you were excited about being part of Cindy's fabulous life.*

Cindy, of course, resented her being there. *Riding on her coat-tails,* she'd called it. Natasha was unaware that she'd said it out loud until Leo flicked a gruff-toned, 'Did you say something?'

'No,' she mumbled—but it was exactly what she'd let herself become: a pathetic hanger-on riding on the coat-tails of her sister's glorious popularity.

Meeting Rico had been like rediscovering that she was a real person in her own right. She'd stupidly let herself believe he had actually fallen in love with her in her own right and not just because of whom she was attached to.

What a joke, she thought now. What a sick, rotten joke.

Rico with Cindy...

Hurt tears scalded the back of her throat.

Rico doing with Cindy what he had always held back from doing with her...

'Oh,' a thick whimper escaped.

'OK?' the man beside her shot out.

*Of course I'm not OK!* Natasha wanted to screech at him. *I've just witnessed my fiancé bonking the brains out of my sister!*

'Yes,' she breathed out.

Leo brought his teeth together with a steel-edged slice. He flashed her a quick glance to find that she was still sitting there with her head dipped and her slender white fingers knotted together on top of her bag.

Had Rico ever taken this woman across his desk the way he'd been having her sister?

As if she could hear what he was thinking, her chin lifted upwards in an oddly proud gesture, her blue eyes staring directly in front. She possessed the flawless profile of a chaste Madonna, Leo found himself thinking. But when he dropped his eyes to her mouth, he was reminded that it was no chaste Madonna's mouth. It was a soft, very lush, very sexy mouth with a short, vulnerable upper lip and a fuller lower lip that just begged to be—

That sudden burn grabbed hold of him right where it shouldn't—residue from what had happened to him as he'd travelled down in the lift, he stubbornly informed himself.

But it wasn't, and he knew it. He had been fighting a hot sexual curiosity about Natasha Moyles from the first time he'd met her at her and Rico's betrothal party. Her sister had been there, claiming centre stage and wowing everyone with her shimmering star quality, wearing a flimsy flesh-coloured dress exclusively designed for her to show off her stem-like figure and her big hairstyle that floated all around her exquisite face, accentuating her sparkling baby-blue eyes.

This sister had worn classic black. It had shocked him at the time because it was supposed to be Natasha's party yet she'd chosen to wear the colour of mourning. He remembered remarking on it to her at the time.

One of his shoulders gave a small shrug. Maybe he should not have made the comment. Maybe he should have kept his sardonic opinion to himself, because if he had done it to get a rise out of her, then he'd certainly got one—of buttoned-lipped, cold-eyed ice.

They'd exchanged barely a civil word since then.

So, she'd taken an instant dislike to him, Leo acknowledged with a grimace that wavered towards wry. Natasha didn't like tall, dark Greeks with a blunt, outspoken manner. He didn't like loud pop-chicks with stick figures and big hair.

He preferred his woman with more softness and shape.

Rico didn't.

Natasha had both.

Leo frowned as he drove them across the river. So what the hell *had* Rico been doing with Natasha, then? Had the stupid fool started out by playing a game with one sister to get him access to the other one, only to find he'd got himself embroiled too deep? Natasha wasn't the type you messed around with. She just would not understand. Had his bone-selfish stepbrother discovered a conscience somewhere between hitting on Natasha and asking her to marry him within a few weeks?

If so, the bad conscience had not stretched far enough to make him leave the other sister alone, he mused grimly as he shot them through a set of lights on amber and spun the car into a screeching left turn.

'Where are you going?' Natasha burst out sharply.

'My place,' he answered.

'But I don't want—'

'You prefer it if I drop you off at your apartment?' Leo flicked at her. 'You prefer to sit nice and neat on a chair with the ba on your lap waiting for them to appear and beg you to forgive?

His English was failing, Leo noticed—but not enoug

to mask the sarcasm from his voice that managed to shock even him.

'No,' she quivered out.

'Because they will appear,' he persisted nonetheless. 'She needs you to keep her life running smoothly while she struts about playing the pop-chick with angst. And Rico needs you to keep his mama happy because Angelina likes you, and she sees you as her precious boy's saviour from a life of wild women and booze.'

Was that it? Had Rico been using her to appease his old-fashioned mother who'd taken a liking to her on sight? Natasha felt hot tears fill her eyes as she replayed the relieved smile Angelina had sent her when they'd happened to bump into her at a restaurant one night. 'Such a nice girl,' Angelina had said later.

Was that the moment when Rico decided that it might be a good idea to make her his wife? He'd asked her to marry him only a few days later. Like a fully paid-up idiot, she had jumped at the chance. They'd barely shared a proper kiss by then!

And no wonder. She wasn't Rico's type, she was *his mother's* type. Cindy was Rico's type.

Her heart hurt as she stared out of the car window. Beside her, Leo felt the truth hit him hard in the gut.

He had his answer as to what had made Rico want to marry this sister while lusting after the other one. He was keeping his mother happy because Angelina had been making stern warning noises about his lifestyle and Rico saw his loving mama as his main artery source to the Christakis coffers—next to Leo himself, of course.

Which made Natasha Rico's love stooge as much as Leo was his family stooge. From the day eight years ago when his father had brought Angelina home as his new bride with her eighteen-year-old son in tow, Leo's life had become round after round of making Rico feel part of the family because Angelina was so hypersensitive to the differences between the two sons. And his father would do anything to keep Angelina happy and content. When Lukas died so suddenly, Leo continued to keep Angelina, via Rico, happy because she'd been so clearly in love with his father and naturally devastated by his death.

Well, not any longer, he vowed heavily. It was time for both Angelina and Rico to take control of their own lives. He was sick and tired of sorting out their problems.

And that included the money Rico had stolen from him, Leo determined, a black frown bringing his eyebrows together across the top of his nose because he'd allowed himself to forget the reason he'd gone into Rico's office in the first place.

Natasha was yet another of Rico's problems, he recognised, winging another swift, frowning glance her way. She was sitting there with her face turned the colour of parchment, looking as if she might be going to throw up in his car.

What, *this* woman? he then cruelly mocked. This ultra composed creature would rather choke on her own bile than to allow herself to do anything so crass as to throw up on his Moroccan tan leather.

Which then brought back the question—what had such a dignified thing seen in a shallow piece of manhood like Rico?

Fresh anger tried to rip a hole in his chest.

'Think about it,' he gritted, wishing he could keep his mouth shut, but finding out he could not. 'They are more suited to each other than you and Rico. He famously likes them like your sister—surely you must have known that, heard some of his history with women? He's been playing the high-rolling playboy right across fashionable Europe for long enough. Did you never stop to ask yourself what it was he actually saw in you that made you stand out from the flock?'

The hurt tears gathered all the stronger at his ruthless barrage. Feeling as if she'd just been knocked over by a bus then kicked for daring to let it happen, 'I thought he loved me,' Natasha managed to push out.

'Which is why he was enjoying your sister over his desk when he should have been attending my board meeting, defending himself.'

'Defending?' she picked up.

Leo didn't answer. Clamping his lips together, he climbed out of the car, annoyed with himself for wanting to beat her up for Rico's sins. Rounding the car bonnet, he opened her door, then reached in to take hold of one of her wrists so he could tug her out, even though he knew she didn't want to get out. Her phone started ringing again, distracting her long enough for him to get her into his house.

He pulled her into the living room and pushed her down into a chair then strode off to the drinks cabinet to pour her a stiff drink.

His hands were trembling, he noticed, and frowned as he splashed neat brandy into a glass. When he walked back to Natasha, he saw that she was sitting on the edge of the chair, all neat and prim with the bag on her lap as he'd predicted she would do.

Fresh anger ripped at him. 'Here.' He handed her the glass. 'Drink that, it might help to loosen you up a bit.'

What happened next came without any warning at all that he was about to receive his just desserts when Natasha shot to her feet and launched the full contents of the glass at his face.

'W-who do you think you are, Mr Christakis, to *dare* to think you can be this horrid to me?' she fired up. 'Listening to you, anyone would be f-forgiven for thinking that it had been *you* who'd been betrayed back there! Or is that it?' she then shot out. 'Are you being this downright nasty to me because you wished it *had* been you doing *that* with my sister instead of Rico—is that what your foul temper is about?'

Standing there with brandy dripping down his hard golden cheekbones, Leo Christakis, the dynamic and cut-throat head of one of the biggest companies in the world, heard himself utter…

'No. I wished it had been you with me.'

# CHAPTER TWO

IN THE thick, thrumming silence that followed that mind-numbing declaration, Natasha stared up at Leo's liquor-drenched face—and wished that the brandy were still in the glass so she could toss it at him again!

'H-how dare you?' she shook out in tremulous indignation, eyes like sparkling blue diamonds darkening to sultry sapphires as the tears filled them up. 'Don't you think I've been h-humiliated enough without you poking fun at me as if it's all been just a jolly good joke?'

'No joke,' Leo heard himself utter, then grimaced at the full, raw truth in his answer. There was definitely no joke to find anywhere in the way he had been quietly lusting after Natasha for weeks.

No, the real joke here was in hearing himself actually admit to it.

Turning his back on her, Leo dug a hand into his jacket pocket to retrieve the never-used handkerchief his various housekeepers always insisted on placing in his suits. Wiping the brandy from his face, he flicked a glance at the way Natasha was standing there in her neat blue suit and her sensible heeled shoes but with her very expressive eyes now blackened by shock.

'You have a strange idea about men, Natasha, if you believe that the scraped-back hair and the buttoned-up clothes stop them from being curious about what it is you are attempting to hide.'

She blinked at him.

Leo laughed—oddly.

'We don't all go for anorexic pop-stars barely out of the schoolroom,' he explained helpfully. 'Some men even like a challenge in a woman instead of seeing it all hanging out and handed to us on a plate.'

His gaze dropped to the rounded shape of her breasts where they heaved up and down inside her jacket. It was pure self-defence that made her pull in her chest. His eyes darkened as he flicked them back to her face and Natasha knew then what it was he was talking about.

'You want to unwrap yourself and fulfil my curiosity?' he invited. 'I didn't think so.' He smiled at her drop-jaw gasp.

'Why are you doing this—s-saying these things to me?' she whispered in genuine bafflement. 'Do you think that because you witnessed what I witnessed it gives you the right to speak to me as if I am a slut?'

'You would not know how to play the slut if your life depended on it,' Leo grimly mocked. 'It is a major part of your fascination to me that with a sister like yours, you are like you are.'

Natasha just continued to stare at him, trying to work out what it was she must have done to deserve any of this. 'Well, you are being loathsome,' she murmured finally. 'And there is nothing in the least bit fascinating about being that, Mr Christakis.'

Her bag had fallen to the floor when she'd jumped to her feet. Natasha bent to recover it, then with as much dignity as she could muster, she turned to leave.

'You're right,' he responded.

'I know I am.' She nodded, taking a shaky step towards the door, and heard him suck in his breath.

'All right,' he growled. 'I'm sorry. OK?'

For mocking her situation just to get the clever quips in?

Straightening her trembling shoulders, 'I didn't ask you to bring me here,' Natasha pushed out in a thick voice. 'I have never asked you to do anything for me. So my sister is a slut. Your stepbrother is a slut. Other than that you and I have nothing in common or to say to each other.'

With that she took another couple of steps towards the door, just wanting to get out of here as quickly as she could do now and willing her legs to continue to hold her up while she made her escape.

Her mobile phone started ringing.

It was like chaos arriving to further agitate havoc because yet another telephone started ringing somewhere else in the house and Natasha's feet pulled her to a confused standstill, the sound of those two phones ringing shrilly in her head.

Behind her *he* wasn't moving a muscle. Was he—was Leo Christakis really as attracted to her as he'd just made out? Her jangling brain flipped out.

Then a knock sounded on the door and the handle was turning. Like a switch that kept on flicking her brain from one thing to another, Natasha envisaged Rico about to walk in the room and her feet were taking a stumbling step back. Maybe she swayed, she didn't know, but a pair of hands arrived to clasp her upper arms and the next thing she knew she was being turned around and pressed against Leo Christakis's shirt front.

'Steady,' his low voice murmured.

Natasha felt the sound resonate across the tips of her breasts and she quivered.

'Oh, I'm sorry, Mr Christakis,' a female voice exclaimed in surprise. 'I heard you come in and assumed you were alone.'

'As you see, Agnes, I am not,' Leo responded.

Blunt as always. His half-Greek housekeeper was used to it, though her eyes flicked curiously to his stepbrother's fiancée standing here held against his chest. When Agnes looked back at his face, not a single hint showed in her expression to say that what she was seeing was a shock.

'Mr Rico keeps ringing, demanding to speak to Miss Moyles,' the housekeeper informed him.

Natasha quivered again. This time he soothed the quiver by tracking a hand down the length of her spine and settling it in the curvy hollow of her lower back. 'We are not here,' Leo instructed. 'And no one gets into this house.'

'Yes, sir.'

The housekeeper left the room again, leaving a silence behind along with a tension that grabbed a tight hold on Natasha's chest. Just totally unable to understand what it was she was feeling any more, she took a shaky step away from him, confused heat warming her cheeks.

'Sh-she's going to think w-we—'

'Agnes is not paid to think,' Leo cut in arrogantly and moved off to pour another brandy while Natasha sank weakly back down into the chair.

'Here, take this…' Coming to squat down in front of her, he handed her another glass. 'Only this time try drinking it instead of throwing it at me,' he suggested. 'It is supposed to be better for you that way.'

His dry attempt at humour made Natasha flick him a brief guilty glance. 'I'm sorry I did that. I don't even know why I did.'

'Don't worry about it.' Leo's smile was sardonic. 'I am used to having my face slapped in car parks and drinks thrown at me. Loathsome guys expect it.'

He added a grimace.

Natasha lowered her eyes to watch his mouth take on that grimacing tilt. It was only as she watched it settle back into a straight line again that she realised it was actually a quite beautifully shaped mouth, slender and firm but—nice.

And his eyes were nice, too, she noticed when, as if drawn by a magnet, she looked back at them. The rich, dark brown colour was framed by the most gorgeous thick, curling black eyelashes that managed to add an unexpected appeal to his face she would never have allowed him before. That pronounced bump in the middle of his nose saved his face from being a bit too perfect. A strong face, she decided, hard hewn and chiselled yet very good-looking—if you didn't count the inbuilt cynicism that was there without her actually knowing *how* it was there.

OK, so he was a lot older than her. Older than Rico by eight years, which made him older than her by a very big ten. And those extra years showed in the blunt opinions he had no problem tossing at people—her especially.

But as for his looks, they weren't old. His skin was a warm honey colour that lay smooth against the bones in his face. No age lines, no smile lines, not even any frown lines, though he did a lot of frowning—around her anyway.

Unaware that she was taking short sips at the brandy as she studied him, Natasha let her eyes track the width of his muscled shoulders trapped inside the smooth fit of his jacket, then let them absorb the fact that his torso was very long and lean and tight. When standing up, he was taller than Rico by several inches and his dark hair was shorter, cut to suit the stronger shape of his face.

She was asking for trouble, Leo thought severely as he watched that lush, pink, generous mouth adopt a musing pout while she looked him over as if he were a prime piece of meat laid out on a butcher's slab.

'How old are you, Natasha?' he asked curiously. 'Twenty-six—twenty-seven?'

Her spine went stiff. 'I'm twenty-four!' she iced out. 'And that is just one more insult you've hit me with!'

'And you're counting.' His eyes narrowed.

'Yes!' she heaved out.

With her blue eyes flashing indignation at him she looked pretty damn fantastic, Leo observed as he knelt there, trying to decide what to do next.

He could leap on her and kiss her—strangely enough she seemed to need him to do that. Or he could gently remove the glass she was crushing between her slender fingers, ease her down on her knees in front of him, then encourage her to just get it over with and use his shoulder to have a good weep.

Something twisted inside him—not sexual this time, but an ache of a different kind. Did she know how badly she was trembling? Did she know her slender white throat had to work like crazy each time to swallow some of the brandy and that her hair was threatening to fall free from its knot?

'I th-think I w-want to go home now,' she mumbled distractedly.

To the apartment she shared with her sister? 'Drink the rest of your brandy first,' Leo advised quietly.

Natasha glanced down at the glass she was holding so tightly between her fingers, then just stared at it as if she was shocked to find it there. As she lifted it to her mouth Leo watched her soft lips take on the warm bloom of brandy and the ache inside him shifted back to a sexual ache.

The doorbell rang.

Rico called her name out.

Natasha's head shot up, the brandy glass falling from her fingers to land with a thunk on the carpet, sending brandy fumes wafting up.

'Natasha—' Leo reached out to her, thinking she was going to keel over into a faint.

But once again Natasha Moyles surprised him. He did not need to pull her to her knees because she arrived there right between his spread thighs with her arms going up and over his shoulders to cling to his neck, those vulnerable blue eyes staring up at him with a helpless mix of pleading and dismay.

'Don't let him in,' she begged tensely.

'I won't,' Leo promised.

'I h-hate him. I never want to see him again.'

'I will not let him in,' he repeated gently.

But Rico called out her name again hoarse with emotion and Leo felt her fingernails dig into the back of his neck while the two of them listened to his housekeeper make some stern response.

'My heart's beating so fast I can't breathe properly,' Natasha whispered breathlessly.

A spark of challenge lit Leo's eyes. He should have contained it—he knew that even as he murmured the challenging, 'I can make it beat faster.'

If he'd said it to distract her attention away from Rico, it certainly worked when her mouth parted on a surprised little gasp. Leo raised a ruefully mocking eyebrow, feeling the buzz, the loin heating, sex-charging, *challenging* buzz.

And he leant in and claimed her mouth.

It was like falling into an electrified pit, Natasha likened dizzily as not a single part or inch of her missed out on the high-voltage rush. She'd never experienced anything like it. He crushed her lips to keep them parted, then slid his tongue into her mouth. The sheer shock feel of that alien wet contact stroking across her own tongue made her shiver with pleasure, then stiffen in shock. He did it again and this time she whimpered.

Leo murmured something, then slid his arms around her

so he could draw her closer to him and deepen the kiss. The next few seconds went by in a fevered hot rush. She felt plastered against his muscled torso. She could hear Rico shouting. Something hard and ridged was pushing against her front. The wildly disturbing recognition of what that something was sent her deaf to everything else as her own senses bloomed with an excited sparkle in response.

It was crazy, she tried telling herself. She didn't even *like* Leo Christakis yet here she was *drowning* in the full on power of his heated kiss! In all of her life she had never kissed anyone like this—never felt even remotely like this! It was like throwing herself against a rock only to discover that the rock had magical powers. His hand skated the length of her spine to her waist, then pressed her even closer, at the same time that he increased the pressure on her mouth, sending her neck arching backwards as he used his tongue to create a warm, thick chain reaction that poured through her entire body like silk.

Natasha heard herself groan something. He muttered a very low, sensual rasp in response. Then Rico called out to her again, harsh and angry enough to pierce into her foggy consciousness, and she wrenched her mouth free.

Trembling and panting with her heart pounding wildly, she stared up at this man while her mind fed her an image of the way Rico had been enjoying Cindy across his desk.

As if her sister knew what she was thinking, her phone began to ring in her purse.

The scald of betrayal burned her up on the inside.

'For God's sake, Natasha, let me *talk* to you!' Rico's rasping voice ground out.

*Revenge* lit her up.

Leo saw it happen and knew exactly where it was coming from. Sanity returned to him with a gut-crushing whoosh. She was going to offer herself to him, but did he want her like this, bruised and heartbroken and throbbing with a desire for revenge on Rico, who could easily charge in here and catch them?

As they had walked into Rico's office and caught him.

Natasha leant away from Leo and began unbuttoning her jacket with shakily fumbling, feverish fingers.

Leo released a sigh. 'You don't want to do this, Natasha,' he said heavily.

'Don't tell me what I don't want,' she shook out.

The two pieces of fabric were wrenched apart to reveal a white top made of some stretchy fabric that crossed over and moulded the thrusting fullness of her two tight breasts.

Leo looked down at them, then up into her fever-bright eyes, and wanted to bite out a filthy black curse. As she wrenched the jacket off altogether, he reached out to try and stop her, only to freeze when he read the helpless plea that had etched itself on her paper-white face.

If he turned her down now, the rejection was going to shatter her.

Her smooth white throat moved as she swallowed, those kiss-warmed lips parting so she could whisper out a husky little, 'Please...'

And he was lost, Leo knew it. Even as she took the initiative away from him by winding her arms around his neck again, he knew he was not going to stop this. Lifting his hands up to mould her ribcage, he stroked them down the tight white fabric to the sexy indentation of her waist in an exploring act that rolled back the denials still beating an urgent tattoo in his head.

Her mouth was a hungry invite. Leo raked his hands back up her body again and this time covered the full perfect globes of her breasts. She fell apart on a series of gasps and quivers that sent her body into an acute sensual arch, fingernails digging into his neck again, hair suddenly tumbling free in a glorious roll of fine silken waves down her back. She was amazing, a stunningly complicated mix of prim, straight-lace and pure untrammelled passion with her lily-white skin and her lush parted mouth, and her breasts two sensational mounds that filled his hands and…

The front door slammed.

Rico had gone.

If Natasha recognised what the sound meant she did not make a response. Her eyes still burned into him with the fevered invitation she was offering.

Time to make a decision, Leo accepted grimly. Continue this or put a stop to it?

Then her fingernails dug deeper to pull his mouth back down onto hers and the decision was made for him.

Natasha felt his surrender and took it with a leap of triumph that bordered on the mad. She became aware of the power of his erection pressing against her again, instinct made her move against it. He muttered a low, throaty response and he was suddenly tightening his hold of her and drawing her to her feet. Next he was swinging her up into his arms and carrying her, the kiss still a seething hot fuse that frazzled her brain and had her heart pounding to the beat of his footsteps echoing on oak flooring as he headed across the hall and began climbing the stairs.

It was the moment that Natasha saw a small chink of sanity. Her head went back, rending the kiss apart as she opened her eyes to look deep into Leo Christakis's heavily lidded dark eyes before she glanced around her as if she'd been woken up suddenly from a dream.

It was only then that she realised that the hallway was empty. No one was there. No Rico witnessing his betrayed fiancée being carried to bed by her soon-to-be new lover. No housekeeper containing her disapproval and shock.

'Changed your mind now you don't have a witness?' Leo's hard voice swung her eyes back to him again.

He'd gone still on one of the stairs and the look of cold cynicism was back, lashing his skin to the bones in his face.

'No,' Natasha breathed, and she discovered that she meant it. She wanted to do this. She wanted to be carried to bed and made love to by a man who genuinely wanted her—she wanted to lose every single old-fashioned and disgustingly outmoded inhibition she possessed!

'Please,' she breathed softly as she leant in to brush a kiss across the hard line of his mouth. 'Make love to me, Leo.'

There was another moment of hesitation, a glimpse of fury in the depths of his eyes. Then he was moving again, allowing her to breathe again though she had not been aware of holding her breath. He finished the climb up the stairs and carried her into a sultry summer-warmed bedroom with pale walls and big dark pieces of furniture. A red Persian rug covered most of the polished oak floor.

Then he really shocked her by dumping her unceremoniously on the top of a huge soft bed.

As Natasha lay there blinking up at him Leo stood looking down at her, his expression as hard and cynical as hell. 'Stay there and pull yourself together,' was all he uttered before he turned around to walk back to the door.

'Why?' Natasha shook out.

'I will not play substitute to any man,' the cold brute answered.

Natasha sat up. 'Y-you said you wanted me.'

'Strange—' he turned, his kiss-heated mouth taking on a scornful twist '—but seeing you getting off on the possibility of Rico witnessing us together was a real turn off for me.'

Natasha sat up with a jolt. 'I was not getting off on it—!'

'Liar,' he lashed back, then really startled her by striding back to the bed to come and lean over her—close enough to make her blink warily because she just didn't know what was going to come next.

'To keep things clear between us, Natasha,' he murmured silkily, 'if you loved what we were doing downstairs so much you forgot all about Rico, then ask yourself what that tells me about Miss Betrayed and Broken-hearted, hmm—?'

It was as good as a cold, hard slap in the face. Natasha just stared up at him because the worst thing of all was that he had only told it how it was! She *had* been thinking about Rico when she'd invited what she had downstairs. And she had *no* excuse for the way she had begged him to bring her up here!

But had he behaved any better? 'You cruel, h-hateful swine,' she breathed, and pulled up her knees so she could bury her face.

Leo agreed. He was behaving like an absolute beast feeding her all the blame for whatever had erupted in *both* of them downstairs. It was still erupting inside him, he admitted as he turned away again and strode back to the door, wishing that he had stayed in Athens this morning instead of...

Telephones started ringing again, piercing through the high-octane atmosphere—his phone in his jacket pocket and another phone ringing somewhere else in the house. Retrieving his mobile, Leo glared at the display screen, expecting it to show Rico's name.

But it was Juno, his PA. Leo sanctioned the connection. 'This had better be important,' he warned as he stepped out of the bedroom and pulled the door shut.

Natasha lifted her head at the sound of the door snapping into its housing. He'd gone. He'd left her sitting here in a huddle on his bed and just walked away from her—because he could.

On a sudden pummelling punch of self-hatred she scrambled up off the bed, hurt beyond sense that yet another man had humiliated her in the space of one horrible day.

Oh, she had to get out of here! Natasha almost screeched that need at herself as she looked around the floor for her shoes and couldn't find them. Then she remembered the vague echo of them falling off her feet and hitting the floor when Leo had picked her up. Her hair fell forward, tumbling in long waves around her face as if to taunt how she'd been so wrapped up in what she'd been doing with him that she hadn't even noticed before now how her hair had sprung free of its restraints!

Like herself. She shuddered, turning like a drunk not knowing where she was going and heading for the door. She made it out onto the landing and even found her way back down the stairs without coming face to face with anyone else. The door to the living room still hung wide-open and the wretched tears almost broke free when she saw the way her jacket lay in a pale blue swish of fabric on the floor by the chair she had been sitting on before she…

Swallowing, she hurried forward to snatch up the offending garment, pulling it on and fastening it up while she scrambled her feet into her shoes.

*He* arrived in the doorway, lounging there and filling it with his lean, dark, overbearing presence and…

Her phone started to ring in her purse.

With what tiny bit of control she had left, Natasha bent down to scoop up the purse, then dragged the phone out with trembling fingers and just slammed the wafer-thin piece of shiny black plastic forcefully down on the floor.

It stopped ringing.

The sudden rush of silence throbbed like the beat of a drum in her head, and the tears were really threatening now like hot, sharp shards of flaming glass hitting the backs of her eyes and her throat. She spun towards the door to find Leo was still there, blocking her only exit.

Her mouth began to work, fighting—fighting the tears. 'Please,' she pushed out at him on a thick broken whisper. 'I need you to move out of my way so I can leave.'

Silence. He said nothing. He did not attempt to move. His eyes were half hooded, his lips straight and tight. And there was just enough narrow-eyed insolence in the way he was casually standing there with his arms folded across his front like that to make Natasha realise that something about him had altered dramatically.

'W-what—?' she shook out.

Leo wondered how she would react if he accused her of being a play-acting little thief?

'I am just curious,' he posed very levelly. 'Leave here for where?'

But inside he didn't feel level in any other way. Inside he was feeling so conned he didn't know how he was managing to hold it all in!

Rico's little accomplice—who would have thought it? Apparently Miss Cool and Prim was not so prim when it came to letting her greedy, grasping, slender fingers scoop up the cash Rico had stolen from him!

'To find Rico, perhaps?' he suggested when she didn't say anything.

'No!' She even managed to shudder. 'H-home,' she said, 'to my apartment.'

'You don't have your keys.'

'I'll get the janitor to let me in.'

'Or your loving sister,' Leo provided. 'I predict she is already there, waiting to pounce on you the moment that you arrive.'

Was the other sister in on the scam, too?

And look at this one, he thought as he shuttered his eyes that bit more before running them down her front. She was back to being buttoned up to the throat as if the passionate interlude they'd just shared had never taken place—if you didn't count the flowing hair and the flush on her cheeks and the kiss-swollen bloom on her lips that he had put there.

'What does it matter to you if she is?' Natasha asked. 'This was never your problem,' she informed him stiffly. 'You should not have become involved. I don't even know why you did *or* why you had to bring me here at all!'

'You needed a safe place to recover,' Leo said dryly.

*'Safe?'* Natasha choked out. 'You'd barely dragged me through your front door before you were coming on to me!'

His careless shrug shot Natasha into movement, wanting, *needing* to get away from the insufferable devil so badly now she was prepared to risk the feeble strength in her shaky legs to walk towards him—aware of the way his eyes followed her every footstep—aware that at any second now she was going to fall down in a screaming hot puddle of tears on the floor.

And *still* he did not move out of her way so she could get out of here, so the closer she came to him, the more her senses went wild, fluttering in protest in case he dared to touch her again—and at the same time fizzing with excitement in the hope that he did!

*I don't know myself any more*, Natasha thought helplessly. 'Move,' she demanded, resorting to a bit of his own blunt way of speech.

The slight tug his mouth gave was an acknowledgement of it, but he didn't shift. 'You cannot leave,' he coolly informed her.

Was he mad? 'Of course I can go.' Shoulders tense, Natasha tried to push him out of her way by placing her hands on his chest. It didn't happen. It was like trying to move a fully grown tree, and in the end Leo caught up her fingers to lift them away from his chest.

'When I said you cannot leave, Natasha, I meant it,' he informed her very seriously. 'At least not until the police arrive to take you away, that is...'

# CHAPTER THREE

Natasha froze for a second. Then, 'The police?' she edged out blankly.

'The Fraud Squad, to be more accurate,' Leo confirmed.

'Fraud…?'

His mouth gave a twitch at the way she kept on echoing him. 'As in swindler and charlatan,' he provided, driving his gaze down her body as if to say the crime was that she looked the way she did yet could turn on so hotly the way she had.

Natasha quivered, her cheeks turning pink with shamed embarrassment. 'I don't usually…'

'Turn on for a man just to pull the wool over his eyes…?'

Untangling her fingers from his, she fell back a couple of steps and really looked at him, catching on at last that he was leading somewhere with this that she was not going to like.

'Since I don't have a single clue what it is you're trying to get at, I think you had better explain,' Natasha prompted finally.

'Does that mean you *do* want to go to bed with me and it is not a sham act?'

Natasha tensed, lips parting then closing again, because the true answer to that taunt was just not going to happen. 'I was in shock when I—'

'In a state of fright, more like,' he interrupted, 'as to what

Rico had done to all your plans, with his crass bit on the desk today.'

'Plans for what?' Lifting a hand into her hair, she pushed the tumbling mass back from her angrily bewildered face. 'I was planning to marry him—well, there's one plan gone down the tubes,' she choked out. 'And as you've just kindly pointed out to me, I caught him having sex with my own sister—so there's my pride gone the same way along with any love for my sister!' The hand dropped to fold along with the other hand tight across her front. 'Then I surrendered to some mad desire to be wanted by *anybody* and you happened to be in the right place at the right time,' she pushed on, 'but that was just another plan sent off down the tubes when you changed your mind about w-wanting me!'

'And now your carefully creamed nest egg is about to go the same way,' Leo added without a hint of sympathy. 'So I would say that you are having a very bad day, today, Natasha. A very bad day indeed.'

'Nest egg?' Natasha picked up. 'What is it you are talking about now?'

Wearing that smile on his lips that she didn't like, Leo levered himself away from the doorframe and moved away, leaving her to turn and watch as he headed for the drinks cabinet.

He needed something strong, Leo decided as he poured neat whisky into a glass. He took a good slug, then turned back to look at her, 'I have just been talking to my PA,' he enlightened. 'Juno has been very busy investigating where Rico stashed the money he stole from me and has managed to trace it to an offshore bank account in your name, so lose the bemused expression, Natasha. I'm on to you....'

Nothing happened. She didn't gasp, she didn't faint, she didn't jump in with a flood of denials or excuses aimed to defend what it was he was talking about now. Instead, Leo stood there and watched while something cold struck into him because there it was, the dawning of *honesty* taking over her lying, cheating, paling face.

That mouth was still a killer though, he observed—and slammed the glass down, suddenly blisteringly angry with himself for being so easily duped by her *challengingly* prim disguise!

'I think you had better sit down before you fall down,' he advised her flatly.

And she did, which only helped to feed his anger all the more. The flowing-haired witch dropped like a stone into the nearest chair, then covered her guilty face with her light-fingered thieving hands!

Rico had *stolen* the money, Natasha was busily replaying over and over. He'd placed *stolen* money in an offshore bank account in *her* name! One of her hands twisted down to cover her mouth as the nausea returned with a vengeance. In the dragging silence blanketing the space separating them she could feel Leo Christakis's ice-cold anger and blistering contempt beating over her in waves.

If he'd made this declaration yesterday, she would not have believed him. But now, with everything else she'd been forced to look at today, Natasha didn't even see a chink of a question glimmering in the nightmare her mind had become as to whether there had been some kind of mistake.

Everything about Rico had been a lie from start to finish. The way he'd used his looks and his charm and his fabulous blinding-white smile to lure her to him, the way he'd poured soft words of love over her too-susceptible head and refused to make love to her because he wanted to protect her innocence, while all the time he'd been cynically planning to turn her into a thief!

Pulling her fingers away from her mouth, 'I'll give you the money back just as soon as I can access it,' she promised.

'Sure you will,' Leo confirmed. 'Once you have recovered your composure, we will go and see to it straight away.'

That brought her face up, whiter than white now so her eyes stood out bluer than blue. 'But you don't understand. I can't touch it yet.'

'Don't play the broken doll with me next, Natasha,' Leo bit out impatiently. 'It won't alter the fact that you are going to give me my money back now—today.'

'But I can't!' Anxiety shot her quivering to her feet. 'I can't touch it until the day before I was supposed to be marrying Rico! He said it was a tax loophole he'd discovered— that *you* had told him about! He said we had to lock the money up under my name in an offshore account until end of business the day before we marry, then transfer it to another account in our m-married name!'

Leo suddenly exploded spectacularly. 'I do not appreciate you trying to involve my name in your filthy scam!' he bit out at her furiously, 'and telling me stupid lies about access to the money is *not* going to get you out of trouble, Miss Moyles! So cough up the cash or watch me call the damn police!'

In a state of nerve-numbing terror, Natasha backed away as he took two long strides towards her with a murderous expression clamped to his face. The backs of her legs hit the chair she'd just vacated and she toppled back into it. He came to stand over her as he'd done in the bedroom, only this time Natasha put up her hands in an instinctive need to keep him at bay.

Watching her cower in front of him sent Leo into an even bigger rage. 'I don't hit women,' he rasped, then turned on his heel and walked away—right out of the room.

The police—he's going to call the police! Out of her mind with fear now, Natasha scrambled upright and chased after him, terrified of going anywhere near him but even more terrified of what would happen if she didn't stop him from carrying out his threat! He'd crossed the hall and entered a room opposite, which turned out to be a book-lined study.

Coming to a jerky halt in the doorway, she stared as he strode up to the desk and picked up the phone.

Panic sent her heart into overdrive. 'Leo, please…' The pleading quaver in her voice made him go still, wide shoulders taut. 'You have got to believe me,' she begged him. 'I didn't know the money was stolen! Rico conned me into banking it for him as much as he conned you out of it in the first place!'

The last part didn't go down too well because he began stabbing numbers into the telephone with a grim resolve that sent Natasha flying across the room to grab hold of his arm.

Warm, hard muscles bunched beneath her clutching fingers, anger and rejection pouring into his muscular frame. 'He s-said it was to ensure our f-future,' she rushed on unsteadily, 'He said it was a bequeath to him from your father *you* had been holding in trust! He s-said you…'

'Wanted to see the back of him so badly I was prepared to break the law to do it?' Leo suggested when her scramble of words dried up.

'Something like that,' Natasha admitted. Then— Oh, dear God, what had she let Rico do to her? 'Now you are telling me he lied, which means he lied to me about absolutely everything and I—'

The phone went down. Leo turned on her so suddenly Natasha was given no chance to react before she found herself trapped in his arms. His mouth arrived. It took hers with an angry heat that offered nothing but punishment yet she responded—responded to him like a crazy person, clinging and kissing him back as if she'd die if she didn't! When he pulled away again she was limp with shock at her own dizzying loss of control!

'Take my advice,' he rasped. 'Keep with the seduction

theme; it works on me a whole lot better than the innocent pleading does.'

Then his fingers gripped her arms like pincers, which he used to thrust her right away from him, and he was re-establishing his connection with the phone.

Natasha's heart lodged like a throbbing lump of fear in her throat. 'Please,' she begged him, yet again having to swallow to be able to speak at all. 'I did not know that Rico had stolen your money, Leo! I can give you back every penny in six weeks if you'll only wait, but, please—*please* don't ring the police—think of the effect it will have on Rico's mother if you have him arrested! She will—'

'You love the bastard,' Leo bit out roughly. Cutting into what she had been trying to say and making Natasha blink.

'At first, y-yes,' she admitted it. 'He flattered me and...' she swallowed again '...and I know it sounds pathetic but I fell for it because...'

Oh, because she'd been a blind fool! She knew it—probably *everyone* knew it!

'Because things were becoming really bad between me and Cindy and I think I was unconsciously searching for a way out.'

Rico had provided it. It was easier to believe she'd fallen in love with him than to admit to herself that she was so unhappy with her life that she'd grabbed the first opportunity handed to her to get out of it without having to cause ructions within her family. It had been so easy to turn blind eyes to what Rico was really like.

She was a coward, in other words, unwilling to take control of her own life without a nice acceptable prop with which to lean upon as she did.

'I'd already realised Rico wasn't w-what I wanted,' she forced herself to go on. 'I was on my way to tell him so today when we—when we caught him with Cindy. It was—'

'Juno…'

Natasha blinked as Leo's voice cut right through what she had been trying to tell him.

'Put a stop on your investigation of Miss Moyles,' he instructed. 'There has been a—mistake. Have my plane for Athens put on standby and add Miss Moyles's name to the passenger list.'

The phone went down. Natasha tugged in a tense breath. 'Why did you say that?'

'Why do you think?' He turned a hard look on her. 'I want my money back and since you've just told me it will be six weeks before you can give it back to me, I am not letting you out of my sight until you do.'

'But I don't want to go to Athens!' Natasha shrilled out. 'I don't want to go anywhere with you!'

'In your present situation that was not the cleverest thing you could say to me right now, Natasha,' Leo said dryly.

'W-what did you mean by that?'

'Sex,' Leo drawled as if that one shocking word were the answer to everything. 'It is your only bargaining chip, so telling me you don't want me is not going to get you out of this sticky situation, is it?'

A sudden dawning as to where he was going with this shot Natasha's trembling shoulders back, sending her loosened hair flying around her face. 'I am not paying you back with sex!' she protested.

'I should think not,' the cold devil answered. 'No woman, no matter how appealingly she presents herself to me, is worth a cool two million to bed.'

'No…' Yet again Natasha found herself sinking into a thick morass of confusion, the intended insult floating right over her as this new revelation struck a blow to her head. 'F-Five hundred thousand pounds,' she insisted through lips so paper dry now it stung to move them. 'Rico opened the account w-with...'

Her voice trailed away when she saw the expression of mocking contempt that carved itself into this man's face. 'Four separate instalments of five hundred thousand adds up to a cool two million—your arithmetic is letting you down,' Leo spelled out the full ugly truth for her.

'Are you sure?' she breathed.

'Grow up, Natasha,' Leo derided the question. 'You are dealing with a real man now, not the weak excuse for a man you fell in love with—'

'I *don't* love him!'

'So here is the deal.' He kept going as if she hadn't made that denial. 'Wherever I go from now on, you will come with me. And to make the pill sweeter for me to take, you will also share my bed as I wait out the six long weeks until you can access *my* money, when you will then hand it back to me before you get the hell out of my life!'

Real skin-crawling panic had to erupt some time because Natasha had been struggling for so long to keep it in. But now the wild need to get away from this ruthless man and the whole situation sent her spinning around and racing out of the room and back across the hall.

Once again she found herself searching for her bag.

'Going somewhere?' that cruel voice mocked her—again.

'Yes.' She dived on the offending article that kept getting away from her without her knowing it had. 'I'm going to find Rico. He's the only person who can tell you the truth.'

'You think I would believe anything he said to me?'

Swinging around, Natasha almost threw her bag at him! 'I will give you back—every single penny of your rotten two million pounds if it kills me trying!' she choked out.

'Euros...'

Leo's smooth drawl sent her still with her blue eyes relaying her next complete daze as to what he was talking about!

'The money will have been converted into Euros,' he pointed out helpfully, then he named the new figure in Euros, freezing Natasha where she stood. 'Of course it means the same when converted back into pounds sterling so long as the exchange rate remains sound, but…' His shrug said the rest for him—that the figure was growing and growing by the minute in the present financial climate. 'And then there is the interest I will charge you for the—loan.'

'I hate you,' was all she could manage to whisper.

'Fortunate for you, then, that you fall apart so excitingly when I kiss you.'

'I need to speak to Rico,' Natasha insisted.

'Still hoping the two of you can escape from this?'

'No!' She shot up her chin, eyes flashing, hair fascinatingly wild around her tense face. 'I need him to tell you the truth even if you do refuse to believe it!'

Leo observed her from an outwardly calm exterior that did not reflect what was crawling around his insides. He was blisteringly angry—with himself more than anyone because he would have been willing to swear that the prim, cool and dignified Natasha Moyles he'd believed he knew had been the genuine article.

No sign of her now, he observed.

'You will have to catch him first,' he told her dryly. 'Juno tells me that Rico has already left the country. He hitched a ride on a friend's private plane out of London airport. He was quicker than you were at realising what was going to come out of his fevered love fest today, you see. A one-minute telephone conversation with Juno after he left here and he knew he'd been sussed. He's left you to carry the can for him, Natasha.' He spelled it out for her in case she had not worked that out for herself.

Feeling as if the whole weight of the world had just dropped onto her shoulders, 'Then you might as well shop me to the Fraud Squad,' she murmured helplessly.

Leo grimaced. 'That is still one way for me to go, certainly,' he agreed, and watched the telling little flinch that she gave up. 'However, you do still have the other way to pull this around, Miss Moyles…' She even flinched at the formal Miss Moyles now. 'You could still try utilising the only asset you have as far as I am concerned and make me an offer I won't want to refuse?'

He was talking sex again. Natasha went icy. 'The money is peanuts to you, isn't it?'

He offered a shrug. 'The difference between the two of us being that I am wealthy enough to call it peanuts, whereas you are not.'

That was so very true that Natasha did not even bother to argue the point. Instead she made herself look at him. 'So you want me to pay the money back with—favours—' for the life of her she could not bring herself to call it *sex* ' and in return you will promise me you will not take this to the police?'

Leo smiled at the careful omission of the word *sex* and for once the smile actually hit the dark of his eyes. 'You do the prim stuff exceptionally well, Natasha,' he informed her lazily as he began to walk towards her, putting just about every defence mechanism she possessed on stinging alert. 'Shame that your hair is floating around your face like a siren's promise and your lips are still pumped up and hot from my kisses, because it forces me to remember the real you.'

Fighting not to flinch when he reached out to touch her, 'I want your promise that if I do what you w-want me to do, you won't go to the police,' she insisted.

His fingers were drifting up her arms. 'You do know you don't have anything left to bargain with, don't you?'

Pressing her lips together, Natasha nodded, her heart pounding in her chest when his fingers reached her shoulders and gripped. 'I'm relying on your sense of honour.'

'You believe I have one?' He sounded genuinely curious.

She nodded again. 'Yes,' she delivered on a stifled breath. She had to believe it because it was the only way she was going to cope with all of this.

He drifted those light caressing fingers along her shoulders until they reached her smooth skin at her nape, making her jump as a long thumb arrived beneath her chin to tilt up her face. His warm, whisky-scented breath had her lips parting like traitors because they knew what was coming next.

'Then you have my promise,' he said softly.

It was the most soul-shrivelling thing Natasha had ever experienced when she fell into that deal-sealing kiss.

Then her mobile phone started ringing, shocking them apart with Natasha turning to stare down at the phone in surprise because she thought she'd killed it when she'd thrown it to the floor.

Leo went to pick it up, since she didn't seem able to move a single muscle, stepping around her and reminding her of a big, sleek giant cat, the way he moved with such loose-limbed grace. Without asking her permission, he sanctioned the call and put her phone to his ear.

It was some fashion designer wanting to know why Cindy had not turned up for a fitting. 'Natasha Moyles is no longer responsible for her sister's movements,' Leo announced before cutting the connection.

Natasha stared up at him in disbelief. 'What did you say that for?'

He turned a mocking look on her. 'Because it is the truth?'

She went to take her phone back. He snatched it out of her way, then slid it into his jacket pocket. 'Think about it,' he insisted. 'You cannot continue play your sister's doormat while you are in Athens with me.'

And just like that he brought the scene in Rico's office pouring back in. Rico hadn't only involved her in his thieving scam, but he'd been treating her like his doormat, too! Natasha turned away, despising herself for being so gullible—despising Rico for making her see herself like this! And then there was Cindy, her loving sister Cindy playing the selfish, spoiled brat who took anything she felt like because she always had done and been allowed to get away with it!

Then another thought arrived, one that hit her like a brick in the chest. Cindy didn't even need Natasha to keep her life running smoothly because arrangements were already in place to hand her singing career over to a professional agency. One of those big, flashy firms with the kind of high profile Cindy had loved the moment its name was mentioned to her. From as early as next week, Natasha would no longer be responsible for Cindy at all, in effect, to free her up to concentrate on her wedding preparations and her move to Milan!

And she'd just found the reason why Cindy had been doing *that* with Rico. Cindy was about to get everything she'd always wanted—a high-profile management team that was going to fast-track her career and more significantly her absolute freedom from the restraints the sister she resented imposed.

She lifted a hand up to cover her mouth. Her fingers were trembling and she felt cold through to the bone.

'What now?' Leo Christakis shot at her.

She just shook her head because she couldn't speak. Cindy being Cindy, she just could not let Natasha walk off into the sunset with her handsome Italian without going all out to spoil it. *I've had your man, Natasha. Now you can trip off and marry him.* She could hear Cindy's voice trilling those words even though they had not yet been said!

Cindy's little swansong. Her wonderful farewell.

'She set me up,' she managed to whisper. 'She knew I was going to meet Rico today so she made sure she got to his office before I did and set me up to witness her doing—that with him.'

'Why would your own sister want to set you up for a scene like that?'

'Because I'm not her real sister.' Natasha slid her fingers away from her mouth. 'I was adopted…' By two people who'd believed their chances of having a child of their own had long passed them by. Five years later and their real daughter had arrived in their arms like a precious gift from heaven. Everyone had adored Cindy—*Natasha* had adored her!

A firm hand arrived on her arm to guide her down into the chair again, then disappeared to collect a second brandy. 'Here,' he murmured, 'take this…'

Natasha frowned down at the glass, then shook her head. 'No.' She felt too sick to drink anything. 'Take it away.'

Leo put the glass down, but remained squatting in front of her as he'd done once before. Strong thighs spread, forearms resting on his knees. His suit, she saw as if for the first time, was made of some fabulously smooth fabric, expensive and creaseless—like the man himself.

And his mouth might look grim, but it was still a mouth she could taste; she felt as if she already knew it far more intimately than any other man's mouth—and that included Rico.

'Stop looking at me as if you *care* what's happening inside my head!' she snapped at the way he was squatting there studying her as if he were really concerned!

He had the grace to offer an acknowledging grimace and climbed back to his full height. So did Natasha, making herself do it, feeling cold—frozen right through, because it had also just hit her that she was on her own now. No sister. No fiancé. Not even a pair of loving parents to turn to because, although they'd loved her in their own way, they had never loved her in the way they loved Cindy. Cindy was always going to come first with them.

'So what is it you want me to do?' she murmured finally in a voice that sounded as cold as she felt.

Leo threw her a frowning dark look. 'I told you what I want.'

'Sex.' This time she managed to name it.

'Don't knock it, Natasha,' Leo drawled. 'The fact that we find we desire each other is about to keep you out of a whole lot of trouble.'

He turned away then, leaving her to stare at his long, broad back. He was so hard she had to wonder who it was that had made him like that.

Then she remembered Rico telling her that Leo had been married once. From what Rico had said, his wife had been an exquisite black-haired, black-eyed pure Latin sex bomb who used to turn men on with a single look. The marriage had lasted a short year before Leo had grown tired of hauling her out of other men's beds and he'd kicked her out of his life for good.

But he must have really loved her to last a whole year with a faithless woman like that. Had his ex-wife mangled up his feelings so badly she'd turned him into the ruthless cynic she was looking at now?

As if he could tell what she was thinking he glanced round at her, catching the expression on her face. Their eyes maintained contact for a few nerve-trapping seconds as something very close to understanding stirred between them, as if he knew what she was thinking and his steady regard was acknowledging it.

'OK, let's go.' Just that quickly he switched from seeming almost human to the man willing to use her for sex until he could get his precious money back. 'Take it or leave it, Natasha,' he cut into the thrumming thick nub of her silence—

there because she was finding the switch much harder to make. 'But make your mind up, because we have a flight to catch.'

A flight to catch. A life to get on with while she put her own on hold—again.

Natasha answered with a curt nod of her head.

It was all he required to have him reach out and pull her back into his arms. The heat flared between them. She uttered a helpless protest as his mouth arrived to claim hers. And worst thing of all was how the whole heady, hot pleasure of it caught hold of her as fast as it took him to make that sensual stroking movement with his tongue along the centre of hers. By the time he drew back, she was barely focusing. Her lips felt swollen and thick—but deep inside, in the core element where the real Natasha lay hidden, she still felt as cold as death.

Leo thought about just saying to hell with it and taking her back upstairs to bed and forgetting about the rest of this. She had no idea—*none* whatsoever—what that hopeless look on her face teamed with the buttoned-up suit was doing to him.

He turned away from temptation, frowning at his own bewildering inclinations. How had he gone from being a tough business-focused tycoon to a guy with his brains fixed on sex?

More than his brains, he was forced to acknowledge when he had to stand still for a moment and work hard to bring much more demanding body parts under control.

Then she moved, swinging him back round to look at her, and he knew then exactly why he was putting this woman before his cool business sense. She had been driving him quietly crazy for weeks now, though he had refused to look at the reason why until Rico had ruined his chances with her.

Rico's loss, his gain. Natasha Moyles was going to come so alive with his tutelage she was not going to be able to hide anything from him. And he was going to enjoy every minute of making that exposure take place. Then once their six weeks were over he would get his money back and walk away so he could get on with his life without having her as a distraction that constantly crept into his head.

Maybe it was worth the cool two million to achieve it.

'I need to speak to m-my parents...'

'You can ring them—from Athens. Hit them with a situation they cannot argue with.'

'That wouldn't be—'

'You prefer to relay the full ugly details to their faces?' he cut in on her. 'You prefer to explain to them that you and Rico have been caught thieving and that their other daughter is a man-thieving tramp?'

The tough words were back. The sigh that wrenched from Natasha was loaded down with defeat. 'I will need to get my passport from the apartment,' was all she said.

'Then let's go and get it.' Leo held out his hand to her in an invitation that was demanding yet another surrender—one that sizzled in the short stillness that followed it.

A step on the road to ruin, Natasha recognised bleakly as she lifted her hand and settled her palm against his. His long tanned fingers closed around her slender cold fingers, she felt his warmth strike through her icy skin and his strength convey itself to her as he turned and trailed her behind him into the hallway, then out of the house.

## CHAPTER FOUR

OUTSIDE the afternoon sunlight was soft on Natasha's face. The short journey to her apartment was achieved in silence. The first thing she saw when they arrived there was Cindy's silver sports car and her aching heart withered, then sank.

Leo must have recognised the car, too, because, 'I'm coming in with you,' he insisted grimly.

It had not been a request. And anyway Natasha was glad she was not going to have to face Cindy on her own.

Feeling dread crawling across her flesh, she walked into the foyer with Leo at her side. The janitor looked up and smiled. It was all she could do to smile politely back by return.

'I've mislaid my keys,' she told him. 'Do you think I could borrow the spare?'

'Your sister is home, Miss Moyles,' the janitor informed her. 'I can call up and she will let you—'

'No.' It was Leo who put in the curt interruption. The janitor looked up at him and it didn't take a second for him to recognise that he was in the presence of a superior power. 'We will take the spare key, if you please.'

And the key changed hands without another word uttered.

In the lift, Natasha began to feel sick again. She didn't want this confrontation. She would have preferred not to look into Cindy's face ever again.

'Do you want me to go in for you?'

The dark timbre of his voice made her draw in a breath before she straightened her shoulders, pressed her tense lips together and shook her head. The moment she stepped into the hi-tech, ultra-trendy living room, her sister jumped up from one of the black leather chairs.

Cindy's eyes were red as if she'd been crying and her hair was all over the place. 'Where have you been?' she shrilled at Natasha. 'I've been trying to reach you! Why didn't you answer your damn phone?'

'Where I've been isn't any of your business,' Natasha said quietly.

Cindy's fingers coiled into fists. 'Of course it's my business. I employ you! When I say jump you're paid to jump! When I say—'

'Get what you came for, *agape mou*,' a deep voice quietly intruded.

Leo's dark, looming presence appeared in the doorway. Cindy just froze where she stood, her baby-blue eyes standing out as hot embarrassment flooded up her neck and into her face. 'M-Mr Christakis,' she stammered out uncomfortably.

Ah, respect for an elder, Natasha noted, smiling thinly as she walked across the room to open the concealed wall safe where she kept her personal papers.

'I didn't expect you to come here....'

Nor had Cindy expected Leo Christakis to catch her with Rico, thought Natasha, and that was why she was embarrassed to see him again.

Leo said nothing, and Natasha winced at the dismissive contempt she could feel emanating from that suffocating silence. Cindy just wasn't used to being looked at like that. She wasn't used to being ignored. Embarrassment and respect changed to a sulky pout and flashing insolence, which she turned on Natasha.

'I don't know what you think you are doing in my safe, Natasha, but you—'

'Be quiet, you little tramp,' Leo said.

Cindy flushed to the roots of her hair. 'You can't speak to me like that!'

Natasha turned in time to watch the way Leo looked her sister over as if she were a piece of trash before diverting his steady gaze to her. 'Got what you need?' he asked gently.

Gentle almost crucified her, though she was way beyond the point of being able to work out why. Fighting the never-far-away-tears, she nodded and made her shaking legs take her back across the room towards him.

Cindy sent her a frightened look. 'You aren't leaving,' she shot out. 'You *can't* leave. That idiot Rico panicked and phoned the parents looking for you—now they're on their way here!'

Natasha ignored her, her concentration glued to the door Leo was presently filling up. *I just need to get away from her, she told herself. I just need to...*

'You're such a blind, silly, stupid thing, Natasha!' Cindy went back on the attack. 'Do you think I'm the only woman Rico has had while he's been engaged to you? Did you really believe that someone like him was going to fall in love with someone like you—?'

Natasha hid her eyes and just kept on walking.

'What are you but the right kind of stuffed-blouse type his silly mother likes? I did you a favour today. You could have married him still blind to what he's really like! It was time someone opened your eyes to reality. You should be thanking me for doing it!'

Natasha had reached Leo. 'Anything else before we get out of here?' he asked.

'S-some clothes and—things,' she whispered.

'Don't you *dare* ignore me!' Cindy screeched. 'The parents will be here in a minute. I want you to tell them that this was all your own fault! I've got a gig tonight and I just can't perform with all of this angst going on. And you need to get busy with some damage control because you won't like it if I have to do it myself!'

Leo stepped to one side to let Natasha pass by him. The moment she closed her bedroom door, he reacted, stepping right up to Cindy. 'Now listen to me, you spoiled little tart,' he said. 'One false word from you about what took place today and you're finished. I will see to it.'

Cindy's head shot up, scorn pouring out of her bright baby blue eyes. 'You don't have the power—'

'Oh, yes, I do,' Leo said. 'Money talks. Jumped up little starlets like you come off a conveyer belt. Give me half an hour with a telephone and I can ruin you so quickly you won't see oblivion until you find yourself sunk in it up to your scrawny neck. Pending records deals can be withdrawn. Gigs cancelled. Careers murdered by a few words fed into the right ears.'

Cindy went white.

'I see that you get my drift.' Leo nodded. 'You are not looking into the eyes of a devoted fan now, sweet face, you're looking into the eyes of a very powerful man who can see right through the shiny packaging to the ugly person that lurks beneath.'

'Natasha won't let you do anything to h-hurt me,' Cindy whispered.

'Yes, she will,' Natasha said. She was standing just inside the door with a hastily packed bag at her feet.

As Cindy looked at her Natasha twisted something out of her fingers, sending it spiralling through the air. It landed with a clink on the pale wood floor at Cindy's feet. Looking down, even Leo went still when he saw what it was.

Her ring—her shiny diamond engagement ring. 'That's just something else of mine you haven't tried,' she explained. 'Why don't you put it on and see if it fits you as well as my fiancé did?'

Cindy's appalled face was a picture. 'I didn't want him, and I don't want—that!'

'Well, what's new there?' Natasha laughed, though where the laugh came from she did not have a single clue. 'When have you ever wanted anything once you've possessed it?'

Pandemonium broke out then as their parents arrived, rushing in through the flat door Leo must have left on the latch.

They looked straight at Cindy. They had barely registered that Natasha was even there.

Cindy burst into a flood of tears.

'Oh, my poor baby,' Natasha heard her mother cry out. 'What did that Rico do to you?'

Natasha began to feel very sick again. She stared at the way her two parents had gathered comfortingly around Cindy and felt as if she were standing alone somewhere in outer space.

Then her gaze shifted to Leo standing on the periphery of it all with his steady dark eyes fixed on her painfully expressive face. 'Can we leave now?' she whispered.

'Of course.'

And he was stooping to pick her bag up. As he straightened again his hand made a proprietary curl of her arm and Natasha heard Cindy quaver, 'He's been stalking m-me for weeks, Mummy. I went to see him to tell him to stop it or I would tell Natasha. The next thing I knew he...'

Leo closed the door on the rest. Neither said a single word to each other as they walked out of the apartment and headed for the lift. All the way down to the foyer they kept their silence, all the way out to his car. He drove them away in that same tense silence until Leo clearly could not stand it any longer and flicked a button on his steering wheel to activate his phone.

Natasha recognised the name 'Juno', then nothing as he proceeded to share a terse conversation in Greek.

She kept her eyes fixed on the side window and just let his deep, firm, yet strangely melodious voice wash over her as they drove out of the city and into lush green, rural England. The ugliness of her situation was crawling round her insides, the spin of once-loved faces turning into strangers as they flipped like a rolling film through her head. She didn't know them and, she realised painfully, they did not really know her—or care.

'Do you think they've noticed that you are no longer there yet?'

Realising Leo had finished his telephone conversation and had now turned his attention on her, Natasha lifted a shoulder in an empty shrug. Had they even noticed she was there in the first place? Pressing her pale lips together she said nothing.

A minute later they were turning in through a pair of gates leading to a private airport where, she presumed, Leo must keep his company jet. It took no time at all to get through the official stuff. All the way through it she stood quietly at his side.

So this is it, Natasha told herself as they walked towards a sleek white jet with its famous Christakis logo shining Ionian blue on its side. I'm going to fly off into the sunset to become this man's sole possession.

She almost—almost managed a dry little smile.

'What?' Leo just never missed anything—not even the smallest flicker of a smile.

'Nothing,' she murmured.

'Forget about Rico and your family,' he said harshly. 'You are better off without them. I am the only one you need to think about now.'

'Of course,' Natasha mocked. 'I'm about to become a very rich man's sexual doormat, which has to be quite a hike up from being my family's wimpish doormat and Rico Giannetti's thieving one.'

Leo said nothing, but she could sense his exasperation as he placed his hand on the small of her back to urge her up the flight steps.

The plane's interior gave Natasha an insight into a whole new way of travelling. Breaking free from his touch, she took a couple of steps away from him, then stopped, tension springing along her nerve-ends when she heard the cabin door hiss as someone sealed it into its housing and the low murmur of Leo's voice speaking to someone, though she did not turn around to find out who it was.

This wasn't right. None of it was right, a sensible voice in her head tried to tell her. She should not be on this plane or tripping off to Athens with Leo Christakis—she should be staying in England and fighting to clear her name!

'Here, let me take your jacket.' He arrived right behind her again, making her whole body jerk to attention when his hands landed lightly on her shoulders.

'I would rather keep it on,' she insisted tautly.

'No, you would not.' Sliding his fingers beneath the jacket collar, he followed it around her slender white throat until he located the top button holding her jacket fastened. 'You will be more comfortable without it.' He twisted the button free.

'Then I can do it.' Snapping up her hands, Natasha grabbed his wrists with the intention of pulling his hands away. He didn't let her.

'My pleasure,' he murmured smoothly as the next button gave.

Her two breasts thrust forward, driving a shaken gasp from her throat. 'I wish you would go and f-find someone else to torment,' she breathed out sharply when his knuckles grazed her nipples on their way to locate the next button, and felt her stomach muscles contract as he brushed across them, too.

He just laughed, low and huskily. 'When did you find the time to stick your hair up again?'

'At the flat,' she mumbled, then went as taut as piano wire when the last button gave way to his working fingers.

'You're too skittish,' he chided.

'And you're too sure of yourself!' Natasha flicked out.

'That's me,' he admitted casually, moving his hands down her sleeves to locate her handbag still clutched in one tense set of fingers. He gently prised it free to toss it aside.

Why the loss of her purse should make her feel even more exposed and under threat, Natasha did not have a clue, but by the time he'd eased the jacket from her shoulders she was more than ready to dissolve into panic. And the worst part about it was that she could not even say for sure any more what it was she was panicking about—Leo and his relentless determination to keep her balanced on the edge of reason, or herself because her senses persisted in responding to him even when her head told them to stop!

His hands arrived at the curve of her slender ribcage, over the stretchy white fabric that moulded her so honestly it felt as if he were touching her skin. Natasha closed her eyes and prayed for deliverance when he eased her back against him and she felt his heat and his hard masculine contours.

'Leo, please...' It came out somewhere between a protest and a breathless plea.

It made no difference. He lowered his mouth and brushed his lips across the exposed skin at her nape and for Natasha it was like stepping off a cliff, she fell that easily. She murmured a pathetic little stifled groan and her head tipped downwards, inviting the gentle bite of his teeth. As he began kissing his way round her neck, she rolled it sideways on a slow and pleasurable, sensual stretch to give him greater access. She so loved what he was making her feel.

'Mmm, you feel good, like warm, living silk to touch,' he murmured. 'You have a beautiful body, Natasha,' he added huskily, gliding his hands upwards until he cupped her breasts and gently pressed his palms against their tightly budded peaks. 'I need you to turn your head and kiss me, *agape mou*,' he told her huskily.

And she did. She moved on a restless sigh of surrender when he reached for her hands and lifted them upwards, then clasped them around the back of his neck. The sheer sensual stretch of her body felt unbelievably erotic. She whispered something—even she didn't know what it was—then she was giving in and twisting her head and going in search of his waiting mouth.

Leo gave it to her in a hot, deep, stabbing delivery. Her fingers curled into the black silk of his hair. It was shocking. She didn't know herself like this, all soft and pliable and terribly needy.

'We are cleared for take-off, Mr Christakis,' a disembodied voice suddenly announced.

Leo drew his head back and the whole wild episode just went up in a single puff of smoke. Natasha opened her eyes and found that she couldn't focus. Passion coins of heat burned her cheeks. She became aware of her hands still clinging to his head and slid them away from him, her still-parted mouth closing with a soft burning crush of her warm lips.

'You are quite a bundle of delightful surprises,' she heard Leo mock. 'Once unbuttoned you just let it all flood out.'

And the real horror of it was that he was, oh, so right! Each time he touched her it was the same as losing touch with her common sense and dignity. Acknowledging that had Natasha breaking free of him to wrap her arms tightly around her body, then she just stood there, shaking and fighting to get a grip on herself.

An engine purred into life.

'Take a seat, strap yourself in, relax,' his hatefully sardonic tone invited, and he was stepping around her to stride down the cabin.

Watching him go, Natasha thought she glimpsed a flick of irritation in the way that he moved and kind of understood it. To a man like Leo Christakis the deal had been done, so to have her continue to play it coy annoyed him. From the little she'd heard about his private life, he liked his women with the experience and sophistication to know how to respond positively to his seduction routine, not blow hot then tense and skittish each time he attempted to act naturally with her.

The gap in their ages suddenly loomed. The fact that there was nothing natural at all in the two of them being together picked at her nerves as she chose a seat at random and sat down.

The plane slid into movement. Natasha watched Leo remove his suit jacket to reveal wide, muscled shoulders hugging the white fabric of his shirt. He draped the jacket over the back of the chair in front of the desk, then folded his long body into the seat placed at an angle to her, those muscled shoulders flexed as he locked in his seat belt, then reached out to pull a large stack of papers towards him and sat back to read.

Dragging her eyes away from him, she hunted down her seat belt with the intention of fastening it, but she spied her discarded jacket lying on the seat opposite and on sheer impulse she snatched it up and put it back on, buttoning it shut all the way up to her throat, though she had no idea what, by doing it, she was hoping to prove.

Unless it had something to do with the tight bubble of anger she could feel simmering away inside at the way he was lounging there already steeped in paperwork and putting on a good impression that he had already forgotten she was here, which hit too closely at the way her family had behaved at the apartment.

Ten minutes later they were in the air and his laptop computer was open, his voice that same melodic drone in her ears. A gentle-voiced stewardess appeared at Natasha's side to ask her if she would like something to eat and drink. She knew she wouldn't be able to eat anything right now, but she asked if it was possible for her to have a cup of tea, and the stewardess smiled an, 'of course,' and went away to see to it.

Leo swivelled around in his chair.

He looked at her, narrowing his eyes on the buttoned-up jacket. A new rush of stinging awareness spun through the air.

'It will have to stay off at some point,' he murmured slowly.

Natasha pushed her chin up and just glared.

It was a challenge that made his dark eyes spark and sent Natasha breathless. Then he was forced to turn his attention back to his satellite link, leaving her feeling hot and skittish for a different reason.

For the next three hours he worked at the desk and she sat sipping her tea or reading one of the magazines the stewardess had kindly brought for her. Throughout the journey Leo kept on swinging his chair around to look at her, waiting until she felt compelled to look back at him, then holding her gaze with disturbing dark promises of what lay ahead. Once he even got up and came to lean over her, capturing her mouth with a deep, probing kiss. As he drew away again the top button to her jacket sprang open.

He did it to challenge her challenge, Natasha knew that, but her body still tightened and her breasts tingled and peaked. The next time he turned his chair to look at her the button was neatly fastened again and she refused point blank this time to lift her head up from the magazine.

They arrived in Athens to oven heat and humid darkness. It was a real culture shock to witness how their passage through the usual formalities was so carefully smoothed. And Leo felt different, like a remote tall, dark stranger walking at her side. His expression was so much harder and there was a clipped formality in the way he spoke to anyone. A quiet coolness if he was obliged to speak to her.

Natasha put his changed mood down to the way people constantly stopped to stare at them. When she saw the cavalcade of three heavy black limousines waiting to sweep them away from the airport, it really came down hard on her to realise just how much power and importance Leo Christakis carried here in his own capital city to warrant such an escort.

'Quite a show,' she murmured as she sat beside him in the rear of the car surrounded by plush dark leather while the other two cars crouched close to their front and rear bumpers. Seated in the front passenger seat of this car and shut away behind a plate of thick, tinted glass sat a man Leo had introduced to her as, 'Rasmus, my security chief'. It was only as he made the introduction that Natasha realised how often she'd seen the other man lurking on the shadowy periphery of wherever Leo was.

'Money and power make their own enemies,' he responded as if all of this was an accepted part of his life.

'You mean, you always have to live like this?'

'Here in Athens, and in other major cities.' He nodded.

It was no wonder then that he was so cynical about anyone he came into contact with, it dawned on her. He flies everywhere in his private jet aeroplane, he drives around in private limousines and he has the kind of bank balance most people could not conjure up even in their wildest dreams. And he has so much power at his fingertips he probably genuinely believes he exists on a higher plane than most other beings.

'I never saw it in London,' she said after a moment, remembering that while he'd been in London he had driven himself.

He turned his head to look at her, dark eyes glowing through the dimness of the car's interior. 'It was there. You just did not bother to look for it.'

Maybe she didn't, but… 'It can't have been as obvious there,' Natasha insisted. 'I was used to some measure of security when Cindy was performing but never anything like this—and none at all with Rico.' She then added with a frown, 'Though that seems odd now when I think about who Rico is and—'

He moved, it was barely a shift of his body but it brought Natasha's face around to catch the flash to hit his eyes.

'What?' she demanded.

'Don't ever compare me with him,' he iced out.

Her blue eyes widened. 'But I wasn't—'

'You were about to,' he cut in. 'I am Leo Christakis, and this is *my* life you are entering into with all its restrictions and privileges. Rico was nothing.' He flicked a long-fingered hand as if swatting his stepbrother away. 'Merely a freeloader who liked to ride on my coat-tails—'

Natasha went perfectly pale. 'Don't say that,' she whispered.

'Why not when it is the truth?' he declared with no idea how he had just devastated her by using the same withering words to describe Rico as her sister had used to describe her. 'His name is Rico Giannetti, though he prefers to think of himself as a Christakis, but he has no Christakis blood to back it up and no Christakis money to call his own,' he laid out with contempt. 'He held an office in every Christakis building because it was good for his image to appear as if he was worthy of his place there, but he never worked in it—not in the true meaning of the word anyway.' The cynical bite to his voice sent Natasha even paler as his implication hit home. 'He drew a salary he did little to earn and spent it on whatever took his fancy while robbing me blind behind my back as I picked up the real tabs on his extravagant tastes,' he continued on. 'He is a hard-drinking, hard-playing liar to himself and to everyone connected to him, including you, his betrayed, play-acting betrothed.'

Shaken by his contemptuous barrage, 'Ex-betrothed,' Natasha husked out unsteadily.

'Ex-everything as far as you are concerned,' he pronounced. 'From this day on he is out of the picture and I am the only man that matters to you.'

He had demanded that she put her family out of her head, now he was insisting she put Rico out of her head. 'Yes, sir,' she snapped out impulsively, wishing she could put him out of her head, too!

A black frown scored his hard features at her mocking tone. 'I thought a few home truths at this point will help to keep this relationship honest.'

'*Honest?*' Natasha almost hyperventilated on the breath she took. 'What you're really doing here is letting me know that you expect to control even my thoughts!'

Impatience hit his eyes. 'I do not expect that—'

'You do expect that!'

Leo raked out an angry sigh. 'I will not have Rico's name thrown in my face by you every five minutes!'

Natasha swung round on him in full choking fury. 'I did not throw his name at you—*you* battered *me* with it!'

'That was not my intention,' he returned stiffly.

Twisting on the seat, she glared at the glazed partition. 'You're no better than Rico, just different than Rico in the way you treat people—women!' she shook out with a withering glance across the width of the seat. 'Since we are driving along here like a presidential cavalcade, your loathsome arrogance is one fault I will let you have, but your—'

'Loathsome—again?' he mocked lazily.

It blew the lid off what was left of her temper. 'And utterly, pathetically jealous of Rico!'

Silence clattered down all around them with the same effect as crashing cymbals hitting the crescendo note and making Natasha's heart begin to race. She could not believe she had just said that. Daring another glance at Leo, she could see him looking back at her like a man-eating shark about to go on the attack, and now she couldn't even breathe because the tension between them was sucking what was left of the oxygen out of the luxury confines of the car.

He reacted with a lightning strike. For such a big man he moved with a lithe, silent stealth and the next thing she knew she was being hauled through the space separating them to land in an inelegant sprawl of body and limbs across his lap. Their eyes clashed, his glittering with golden sparks of anger she hadn't seen in them before. Hers were too wide and too blue and—scared of what was suddenly fizzing in her blood.

She had to lick her suddenly very dry lips just to manage a husky, 'I didn't really m-mean—'

Then came the kiss—the hot and passionate ambush that silenced her attempt to retract what she'd said, and flung her instead into fight with lips and tongues and hands that did not know how to stay still. His breath seared her mouth and a set of long fingers was clamped to the rounded shape of her hip, her own fingers applying digging pressure to whatever part of his anatomy they could reach as their mouths strained and fought. The motion of the car and the fact that they were even *in* one became lost in the uneven fight. She wriggled against him. His hand maintained its controlling clamp. She felt her fingernails clawing at his nape and the rock-solid moulding of his chest so firmly imprinted against his shirt.

He loved it. She caught his tense hiss of pleasure in her

mouth and felt a tight, pleasurable shudder attack his front, the powerful surge of his response making itself felt against the thigh he held pressed into his lap. Then his hand was sliding beneath her skirt and stroking the pale skin at the top of her thigh where her stockings did not reach. If he stroked any higher, he was going to discover that she was wearing a thong and she increased her struggle to get free before he reached there, lost the fight, and a quiver of agonising embarrassment sent her kiss-fighting mouth very still.

'Well, what do we have here?' he paused to murmur slowly, long fingers stroking over a smoothly rounded, satin-skinned buttock and crippling Natasha's ability to breathe. 'The prim disguise is really beginning to wear very thin the more I dig beneath it.'

'Shut up,' she choked, eyes squeezed tight shut now. She was never going to wear a thong ever again, she vowed hectically.

He removed his hand and her eyes shot open because she needed to know what he was going to do next, and found herself staring into his mockingly smiling face. The anger had gone and his lazily, sensual male confidence was firmly back in place.

'Any more hidden treasures left for me to discover?' He arched a sleek, dark, quizzing eyebrow.

'No,' Natasha mumbled, which made him release a dark, husky laugh that shimmered right through her as potently as everything else about him did.

Then he wasn't smiling. 'OK, so I am jealous of Rico where you are concerned.' He really shocked her by admitting it. 'So take my advice and don't bring him into our bed or I will not be responsible for the way I react.'

Before she could respond to that totally unexpected backdown, he was lowering his head again and crushing her mouth. How long this kiss went on Natasha had no idea, because she just lost herself in the warm, slow, heady promise it was offering.

The car began to slow.

Both felt the change in speed but it was Leo who broke away and with a sigh lifted her from him to place her back on the seat. Lounging back into the corner of the car, he then watched the way she concentrated on trying to tidy herself, shaky fingers checking buttons and pulling her skirt into place across her knees.

'Miss Prim.' He laughed softly.

Lifting her fingers to smooth her hair, Natasha said nothing, a troubled frown toying with her brow now because she just could not understand how she could fall victim to his kisses as thoroughly as she did.

'It's called sexual attraction, *pethi mou*,' Leo explained, reading her thoughts as if he owned them now.

Her profile held Leo's attention as it turned a gentle pink. If he did not know otherwise, he would swear that Natasha Moyles was an absolute novice when it came to sexual foreplay. She ran from cold to hot to shy and dignified. She was not coquettish. She did not flirt or invite. She appeared to have no idea what she did to him yet she was so acutely receptive to anything that he did to her.

And she made him ache just to sit here looking at her. It was not an unpleasant condition; in fact, it had been so many years since he'd felt this sexually switched on to a woman, he'd believed he had lost the capacity to feel anything quite this intense.

Gianna had done that to him, scraped him dry of so many feelings and turned him into an emotional cynic. But his ex-wife was not someone he wanted to be thinking of right now, he told himself as he focused his attention back on this woman who was keeping his senses on edge just by sitting here next to him.

'We have arrived,' he murmured, using the information like yet another sexual promise to taunt her with, then watched her slender spine grow tense as she glanced beyond the car's tinted glass to catch sight of the twin iron gates that guarded the entrance to his property.

Natasha stared at the gates as they slid apart to their approach. All three cars swept smoothly through them, then two cars veered off to the left almost immediately while theirs made a direct line for the front of his white-painted, three-storey villa.

Rasmus was out of the car and opening Leo's door the moment the car pulled to a stop at the bottom of the curving front steps. Leo climbed out, ruefully aware that his legs didn't feel like holding him up. Desire was a gnawing, debilitating ache once it buried its teeth in you, he mused ruefully as he turned to watch his driver open the other passenger door so the object of his desire could step out of the car.

She gazed across the top of the car up at his villa with its modern curving frontage built to follow the shape of the white marbled steps. Light spilled out of curving-glass windows offset in three tiers framed by white terrace rails.

'I live at the top,' he said. 'The guest suites cover the middle floor. My staff have the run of the ground floor...what do you think?'

'Very ocean-going liner,' Natasha murmured.

Leo smiled. 'That was the idea.'

Rasmus shifted his bulk beside him then, reminding Leo that he was there. Leo glanced at him, that was all, and both Rasmus and the driver climbed back in the car and firmly shut the doors. Then the car moved away, leaving Leo and Natasha facing each other across its now-empty space. It was hot and it was dark but the light from the building lit up the two of them and the exotic scent of summer jasmine hung heavy in the air.

Natasha watched as Leo ran his eyes over her suit and the bag she once again clutched to her front. He didn't even need to say what he was thinking any more, he just smiled and she knew exactly what was going through his head. He was letting her know how much he was looking forward to stripping her of everything she liked to hide behind.

And the worst part about it was that her insides feathered soft rushes of excitement across intimate muscles in expectant response.

When he held out his hand in a silent command that she go to him, Natasha found herself closing the gap between them as if pulled across it by strings.

# CHAPTER FIVE

No MAN had a right to be as overwhelmingly masculine as Leo did, Natasha thought as the feathering sensation increased as she walked. With his superior height, the undeniable power locked into his long, muscled body and that bump on his nose, which announced without apology that there was a real tough guy hiding inside his expensively sleek billionaire's clothes.

He turned towards the house as she reached him, the out-stretched hand becoming a strong, muscled arm he placed across her back, long fingers curling lightly against her rib-cage just below the thrust of her breasts.

Antagonism at his confident manner began dancing through her bloodstream—fed by a fizzing sense of antici-pation that held her breath tight in her lungs. Walking beside him made Natasha feel very small suddenly, fragile, so in-tensely aware of each curve, each small nuance of her own body that it was as close as she'd ever come to experiencing the truly erogenous side of desire.

Inside, the villa was a spectacular example of modern ar-chitecture, but Natasha didn't see it. She was too busy absorb-ing the tingling sensations created by each step she took as they walked towards a waiting lift.

Once she stepped into it she would be lost and she knew it.

So that first step into the lift's confines felt the same to her as stepping off the edge of a cliff. The doors closed behind them. She watched one of Leo's hands reach out to touch a button that sent the lift gliding smoothly up. He still kept her close to him, and she kept her eyes carefully lowered, unwilling to let him see what was going on inside her head. The lift doors slid open giving them access into a vast reception hallway filled with soft light.

The very last thing Natasha wanted to see was another human being standing there waiting to greet them. It interfered with the vibrations passing between the two of them and brought her sinking back to a saner sense of self.

'*Kalispera*, Bernice,' Leo greeted smoothly, his hand arriving at Natasha's elbow to steady her shocked little backwards step.

'Good evening, *kirios—thespinis*,' the stocky, dark housekeeper turned to greet Natasha in heavy, accented English. 'You have the pleasant flight?'

'I—yes, thank you,' Natasha murmured politely, surprised that she seemed to be expected, then blushing when she realised just what that meant.

Bernice turned back to Leo. 'Kiria Christakis has been ringing,' she informed him.

'Kiria Angelina?' Leo questioned.

'*Okhi...*' Bernice switched languages, leaving Natasha to surmise that her ex-future mother-in-law had left a long message to relay her shock and distress, going by the urgency of Bernice's tone.

'My apologies, *agape mou*, but I need a few minutes to deal with this.' Leo turned to Natasha. 'Bernice will show you where you can freshen up.'

His expression was grim and impatient. And despite his

apology he did not hang around long enough for Natasha to answer before he was turning to stride across the foyer, leaving her staring after him.

'Leo...?' Calling his name brought him to an abrupt standstill.

'Yes?' He did not turn around.

Natasha was tensely aware of Bernice standing beside her. 'W-will you tell your stepmother for me, please, that I am truly sorry ab-about the way that—things have worked out?'

His silent hesitation lasted longer than Natasha's instincts wanted to allow for. Beside her, Bernice shifted slightly and lowered her head to stare down at the floor.

'I l-like Angelina,' she rushed on, wondering if she'd made some terrible faux pas in Greek family custom by speaking out about personal matters in front of the paid staff. 'None of what happened was her fault and I know she m-must be disappointed and upset.'

Still, he hesitated, and this time Natasha felt that hesitation prickle right down to her toes.

Then he gave a curt nod. 'I will pass on your message.' He strode on, leaving her standing there feeling...

'This way, *thespinis*...'

Feeling what? she asked herself helplessly as Bernice claimed her attention, indicating that she follow her into a wide, softly lit hallway that led off the foyer.

Bernice showed her into beautiful bedroom suite with yet more soft light spilling over a huge divan bed made up with crisp white linen. Dragging her eyes away from it, Natasha stared instead at a spectacular curving wall of glass backdropped by an endless satin dark sky.

Bernice was talking to her in her stilted English, telling her where the bathroom was and that her luggage would arrive very soon.

Luggage, Natasha thought as the housekeeper finally left her alone. Did one hastily packed canvas holdall classify as luggage?

*Dear God, how did I get to be standing here in a virtual stranger's bedroom, waiting for my luggage?* she then mocked herself, and wasn't surprised when her gaze slid back to that huge divan bed, then flicked quickly away again before her imagination could conjure up an image of what they were going to be doing there soon.

Heart thumping too heavily in her chest, Natasha sent her restless eyes on a scan of the remainder of her spacious surroundings, which bore no resemblance at all to Leo's very traditional Victorian London home. Here, cool white dominated with bold splashes of colour in the bright modern abstracts hanging from the walls and the jewel-blue cover she'd spied draped across the end of the bed.

Needing to do something—anything—to occupy her attention if she didn't want to suffer a mad panic attack, she walked over to the curved wall of glass with the intention of checking out the view beyond it, but the glass took her by surprise when it started to open, parting in the middle with a smooth silent glide—activated, she guessed, by her body moving in line with a hidden sensor.

Stepping out of air-controlled coolness into stifling heat caught her breath for a second, then she was dropping her purse onto the nearest surface, which happened to be one of the several white rattan tables and chairs spread around out there, and she was being drawn across the floor's varnished wood surface towards the twinkle of lights she could see beyond the white terrace railing, while still trying to push back the nervous flutters attacking her insides along with the deep sinking knowledge that she really should not be doing this.

A city of lights suddenly lay spread out beneath her, looking so glitteringly spectacular Natasha momentarily forgot her worries as she caught her breath once more. She'd been aware that they'd climbed up out of the city on the journey here from the airport, but she had not realised they'd climbed as high as this.

'Welcome to Athens,' a smooth, dark, warm velvet voice murmured lightly from somewhere behind her.

She hadn't heard him come into the bedroom, and now tension locked her slender shoulders as she listened to his footsteps bring him towards her.

'So, what do you think?'

His hands slid around her waist to draw her against him. 'Fabulous,' she offered, trying hard to sound calm when they both knew she wasn't by the way she grew taut at his closeness. 'Is—is that the Acropolis I can see lit up over there?'

A slender hand pointed out across the city. When she lowered it again, she found it caught by one of his.

'With the told quarters of Monastiraki and the Plaka below it,' he confirmed, taking her hand and laying it against her fluttering stomach, then keeping it there with the warm clasp of his. 'Over there you can see Zappeion Megaron lit up, which stands in our National Gardens, and that way—' he pointed with his other hand '—Syntagma Square…'

The whole thing turned a bit surreal from then on as Natasha stood listening to his quietly melodic voice describing the night view of Athens as if there were no sexual undercurrents busily at work. But those undercurrents *were* at work, like the tingling warmth of his body heat and the power of his masculine physicality as he pressed her back against him. She felt wrapped in him, trapped, surrounded and overwhelmed by a pulse-chasing vibration of intimacy that danced along her nerve-ends and fought with her need to breathe.

'It is very dark with no moon tonight but can you see the

Aegean in the distance lit by the lights from the port of Piraeus.' She had to fight with herself to keep tuned into what he was saying. 'After Bernice has served our dinner I will show you the view from the other terrace, but first I would like you to explain to me, *pethi mou*, what has changed in the last five minutes to scare you into the shakes?'

'Leo…' Impulsive, she seized the moment. 'I can't go through with this. I thought I could but I can't.' Slipping her hand out from beneath his, she turned to face him, 'I need you to understand that this…'

Her words dried up when she found herself staring at his white-shirted front. He'd taken off his jacket and his tie had gone, the top couple of buttons on his shirt tugged open to reveal a bronzed V of warm skin and a deeply unsettling hint of curling black chest hair.

The air snagged in her chest, the important words—this will be my first time—lost in the new struggle she had with herself as her senses clamoured inside her like hungry beasts. She wanted him. She did not understand why or how she had become this attracted or so susceptible to him but it was there, dragging down on her stomach muscles and coiling around never before awakened erogenous zones.

'We have a deal, Natasha,' his level voice reminded her.

A deal. Pressing her trembling lips together, she nodded. 'I know and I'm s-sorry but—' Oh, God. She had to look away from him so she could finish. 'This is too m-much, too quickly and I…'

'And you believe I am about show my lack of finesse by jumping all over you and carrying you off to bed?'

'Yes—n-no.' His sardonic tone locked a frown to her brow.

'Then what do you expect will happen next?'

'Do you have to sound so casual about it?' she snapped out, taking a step back so her lower spine hit the terrace rail. Discomforted and disturbed by the whole situation, she wrapped her arms across her front. 'You might prefer to believe that I do this kind of thing on a regular basis, but I don't.'

'Ah,' he drawled. 'But you think that I do.'

'No!' she denied, flashing a glare up at him, then wished she hadn't when she saw the cynically amused cut to his mouth. 'I don't think that.'

'Good. Thank you,' he added dryly.

'I don't know enough about you to know how you run your private life!'

'Just as I know little about your private life,' he pointed out. 'So we will agree to agree that neither of us is without sexual experience and therefore can be sophisticated enough to acknowledge that we desire each other—with or without the deal we have struck.'

'But I haven't,' she mumbled.

'Haven't—what?' he sighed out.

Too embarrassed to look at him, cheeks flushed, Natasha stared at her foot. 'Any sexual experience.'

There was one of those short, sharp silences, in which Natasha sucked on her lower lip. Then Leo released another sigh and this one kept on going until it had wrung itself out.

'Enough, Natasha,' he censured wearily. 'I did not come out of the womb a week ago so let's leave the play-acting behind us from now on.'

'I'm not play-acting!' Her head shot up on the force of her insistence. All she saw was the flashing glint of his impatience as he reached out and pulled her towards him. Her own arms unfolded so she could use her hands to push him away again, but by then his mouth was on hers, hot, hard and angrily determined. Her fists flailing uselessly, he drew her into his arms and once again she was feeling the full powerful length of him against her body. Without even knowing it happened she went from fighting to clinging to his shoulders as her parted mouth absorbed the full passionate onslaught of his kiss.

There was no in-between, no pause to decide whether or not she wanted to give in to him, it just happened, making an absolute mockery of her agitation and her protests because Leo was right, and she did want him—badly.

*This* badly, Natasha extended helplessly as he deepened the kiss with that oh-so-clever stroke of his tongue, and she felt her body responding by stretching and arching in sensuous invitation up against the hardening heat of his.

And she knew she was lost even before he put his hands to her hips and tugged her into even closer contact with what was happening to him. When he suddenly pulled his head back, she released a protesting whimper—it shocked even Natasha at the depth of throaty protest it contained.

He said something terse, his eyes so incredibly dark now they held her hypnotised. 'You want me,' he rasped softly. 'Stop playing games with me.'

Before she could answer or even try to form an answer, he was claiming her mouth again and deepening the whole wildly hot episode with a kiss that sealed his declaration like a brand burned into her skin. Her arms clung and he held her tightly against him—nothing, she realised dizzily, was now going to stop this.

And she didn't want it to stop. She wanted to lose herself in his power and his fierce sensuality and the heat of the body she was now touching with greedily restless fingers. She felt the thumping pound of his heartbeat and each pleasurable flinch of his taut muscles as her fingers ran over them. His shirt was in her way—he knew it was in her way and, with a growl of frustration, he stepped back from her, caught hold of her hand and led her back inside.

The bed stood out like a glaring statement of intent. He

stopped beside it, then turned to look at her, catching her uncertain blue stare and leaning in to kiss it away before stepping back again. If there was a chink of sanity left to be had out of this second break in contact, it was lost again by a man blessed with all the right moves to keep a woman mesmerised by him.

He began removing his shirt, his fingers slowly working buttons free to reveal, inch by tantalising inch, his long, bronzed torso with his black haze of body hair and beautifully formed, rippling muscles, which Natasha's concentration became solely fixed on. She had never been so absorbed by anything. Sexual tension stung in the air, quickening her frail breathing as he began to pull the shirt free from the waistband of his trousers. When the shirt came off altogether, she felt bathed in the heady thrill of his clean male scent. He was so intensely masculine, so magnificently built—she just couldn't hold back from reaching out to place her hands on him.

And he let her. He let her explore him as if she was on some magical mystery journey into the unknown, his arms, the glossy skin covering his shoulders, the springy black hair covering his chest. As her hands drifted over him, her tongue snaked out to taste her upper lip, but she knew that really it wanted to taste him.

Leo reached up and gently popped the top button of her jacket and she gasped as if it was some major development, her eyes flicking up to catch his wry smile sent to remind her that this undressing part was a two-way thing. He leant in to kiss her parted lips as he popped the next button, and the whole battle they'd been waging with her jacket took on a power of its own as she just stood there and let him pop buttons between slow, deep, sensuous kisses, until there were no buttons left to pop.

He discarded her jacket in the same way he had discarded it once already that day, without letting up on his slow seduction by making her shiver as he trailed his fingers up her bare arms and over her shoulders, then down the full length of her back, making her arch towards him, making her whisper out a sigh of pleasure, making her eyes drift shut in response. Then he just peeled her stretchy white top up her body and right over her head. Cool air hit her skin and the shock of it made her open her eyes again. He was looking down at her breasts cupped in plain white satin, the fullness of their creamy slopes pushing against the bra's balcony edge. When the bra clasp sprang open and he trailed that flimsy garment away, her hands leapt up to cover her bared breasts. Leo caught her wrists and pulled them away again, his ebony eyelashes low over the intense glow in his eyes now as he watched her nipples form into pink, tight, tingling peaks.

Nothing prepared her for the shot of pleasure she experienced when he drew her against him and her breasts met with his hair-roughened chest.

No turning back now, Natasha told herself hazily as the wriggle of doubts faded away to let in the rich, drugging beauty of being deeply kissed. She felt her skirt give, felt it slither on its smooth satin lining down her legs to pool at her feet. Her bra was gone. The thong was nothing. The fine denier stocking clung to her slender white thighs. Her hair came loose next, unfurling down her naked back like an unbelievably sexy caress.

Leo had all but unwrapped her and she'd never felt so exquisitely aware of herself as a desirable woman. When he drew back from her, she reached for him to pull his mouth back to hers. He murmured something—a soft curse, she suspected—then picked her up and placed her down on the bed. Natasha held on to him by linking her hands around his neck to make sure that the kiss did not break. She wanted him—all of him.

'Greedy,' he murmured softly against her mouth as he stretched out beside her, and she was! Greedy and hungry and caught in the sexual spell he'd been weaving around her for most of the day.

Then one of his hands cupped the fullness of her breast and her breath stalled in her throat as he left her mouth to capture the tightly presented peak. Sensation made her writhe as he sucked gently, her fingers clawing into the thick silk of his hair with the intention of pulling him away—only it didn't happen because his teeth lightly grazed her, and soon she was groaning and clinging as the smooth, sharp feel of his tongue and his teeth and his measured suck drew pleasure on the edge of tight, stinging pain downward until it centred between her thighs.

Maybe he knew, maybe she groaned again, but his mouth was suddenly hot and urgently covering hers. And she could feel the hunger in him, the urgent intent of his desire demanding the same from her and getting it when he kissed her so deeply she felt immersed in its power.

Then he was leaving her, snaking upright and trailing the thong away as he did so. Eyes hooded again, dark features severe now, he removed her stockings, then straightened up to unzip his trousers and heel off his shoes while running his eyes over her possessively.

'You're beautiful,' he murmured huskily. 'Tell me you want me.'

There was no denying it when she couldn't take her eyes off him, no pretending that she was a victim here when her body responded wildly to the sight of his naked power.

'I want you,' she whispered.

It was Natasha who reached for him when he came down beside her again. It was she that turned to press the full length of her eager body into his.

Then he was taking control again, pushing her gently onto her back and rolling half across her. What came next was a lesson in slow seduction. He laid hot, delicate kisses across her mouth, touched her with gentle fingers, caressed her breasts and her slender ribcage, stroking feather-light fingertips over her skin to the indentation of her waist and across the rounded curves of her hips. It was an exploration of the most intense, stimulating agony; her flesh came alive as she moved and breathed and arched to his bidding. When he finally let his hand probe the warm, moist centre between her thighs, she was lost, writhing like a demented thing, clinging to his head and begging for his kiss. And he was hot, he was tense, he was clever with those deft fingers. The new shock sensation of what he was doing to her dropped her like a stone into a whirlpool of hot, rushing uproar.

'Leo,' she groaned out.

Saying his name was like giving him permission to turn up the heat. He appeared above her, big and dark—fierce with burning eyes and sexual tension striking across his lean cheeks. He recaptured her mouth with a burning urgency, shuddering when her fingers clawed into his nape. And still, he kept up the unremitting caresses with his fingers, driving her on while each desperate breath she managed to take made the roughness of his chest rasp torturously against the tight, stinging tips of her breasts.

She could feel the powerful nudge of his erection against her. Her tongue quivered with knowledge against his. A flimsy, rippling spasm was trying to catch hold of her and she whimpered because she couldn't quite seize it.

Leo muttered something thick in his throat, then rose above her like some mighty warrior, so powerfully, darkly, passionately Greek that if she had not felt the pounding thunder of his heartbeat when she sent her hands sliding up the wall of his chest, Natasha could have convinced herself that he just wasn't real.

He eased between her parted thighs with the firm, nude tautness of his narrow hips and the rounded tip of his desire made that first probing push against her flesh. Feeling him there, understanding what was coming and so naïvely eager to receive it, Natasha threw her head back onto the bed, ready, wanting this so very badly she was breathless, riddled by needs so new to her that they held her on the very edge of screaming-pitch.

So the sudden, fierce thrust of his invasion followed by a sharp, burning pain that ripped through her body had her clenching her muscles on a cry of protest.

Leo froze. Her eyes shot to his face. She found herself staring into passion-soaked, burning brown eyes turned black with shock. 'You were a virgin. You—'

Natasha closed her eyes and refused to say anything, while his deriding denial that this would be her first time replayed its cruel taunt across her tense body, and the muscles inside her that were already contracting around him.

'Natasha—'

'No!' she cried out. 'Don't talk about it!'

He seemed shocked by her agonised outburst. 'But you—'

'Please get off me,' she squeezed out in desperation and pushed at his shoulders with her tightly clenched fists. 'You're hurting me.'

'Because you are new to this…' His voice had roughened, the hand he used to gently push her hair away from her face trembling against her hot skin.

But he made no attempt to withdraw from her, his big shoulders bunched and glossed with a fine layer of perspiration, forearms braced on either side of her, and his face was so grave now Natasha knew what was coming before he said it.

'I'm sorry, *agape mou*…'

'Just get off!' She didn't want his apology. Balling her

hands into fists, she pushed at his shoulders, writhing beneath him in an effort to get free, only to flatten out again on a shivering quiver of shock when her inner muscles leapt on his intrusion with an excited clamour that made her eyes widen.

Reading her expression with an ease that pushed a hot flush through her body, 'You are not hurting any more,' he husked out, and lowered his head to adorn her face with soft, light, coaxing kisses—her eyes, her nose, her temples, her delicate ear lobes—that made her quiver and squirm and in the end dig fingers into his bunched shoulders and send her mouth on a restless search for his.

'Oh, kiss me properly!' she ended up begging.

Her helpless plea was all it took to tip a carefully contained, sexually aroused man over the edge. On a very explicit curse, he moulded her mouth to his. A second later and Natasha was lost—flung into a strange new world filled with sensation, piling in on top of sensation, unaware that the whole wild beauty of it was being carefully built upon by a master lover until she felt the first rippling spasm wash through her. She knew that he felt it, too, because he whispered something hot against her cheek, slid his powerful arms beneath her so he could hold her close, then angled his mouth to hers and began to thrust really deep, increasing the pace while maintaining a ferocious grip on his own thundering needs.

The grinding drag of fierce pleasure began to flow through her body. Natasha whimpered helplessly against his mouth. Knotting his fingers into her hair, he muttered tensely, 'Let go, *agape mou*.'

And like a fledgling bird being encouraged to fly, Natasha just opened her sensory wings and dropped off the edge of the world into an acutely bright, scintillating dive straight into the frenzied path of an emotional storm. A moment later she felt him shudder as he made the same mind-shredding leap, while urging her on and on until two became one in a wildly delirious, spiralling spin.

It was as if afterwards didn't exist for Natasha; pure shock dropped her like a rock through a deep, dark hole into an exhausted sleep.

Maybe she did it because she did not want to face what she'd done, Leo mused sombrely as he sat sprawled in a chair by the bed, watching her—watching this woman he'd just bedded like some raving sex maniac while giving himself every excuse he could come up with to help him to justify his behavior.

A virgin.

His conscience gave him a stark, piercing pinch.

And the guilty truth of it was, he could still feel the sense of stinging, hot pleasurable pressure he'd experienced when the barrier gave. A muscle low down in his abdomen gave a tug in direct response to the memory and he lifted the glass of whisky he held and grimly took a large sip.

The prim persona had been no lie.

She even slept the sleep of an innocent, he observed as he ran his eyes over her. No hint of sensual abandon in the modest curve of her body outlined against the white sheet.

Another slug at the whisky and he was studying her face next. Perfect, beautiful, softened by slumber and washed pale by the strain of the day she'd been put through when she should look...

He took another pull of the whisky, and as he lifted the glass to his mouth, her eyelids fluttered upwards and her sleep-darkened blue eyes looked directly at him.

The nagging tug on his loins became a pulsing burn that made him feel like a sinner.

He lowered the glass, and half hiding his eyes, watched her catch her breath, then freeze for a second before he said sombrely, 'We will get married.'

Natasha almost jolted right out of her skin. 'Are you mad?' she gasped, pulling the covering sheet tightly up against her chin. 'We have a deal—'

'You were a virgin.'

As she dragged herself into a sitting position her hair tumbled forwards in a shining, loose tangle of waves around her face and she pushed it out of her way impatiently. 'What the heck difference should that make to anything?'

'It means everything,' Leo insisted. 'Therefore we will be married as soon as I can arrange it. I am honour-bound to offer you this.'

'Stuff your honour.' Heaving in a deep breath, Natasha climbed out of the bed on the other side from where he was sitting, trailing the sheet around her as she went. 'Having just escaped one sleazy marriage by the skin of my teeth, I am *not* going to fall into another one!'

'It will not be a sleazy marriage.'

'Everything about you and your terrible family is sleazy!' she turned on him angrily. 'You're all so obsessed with the value of money, you've lost touch with what's really valuable in life! Well, I haven't.' Tossing her chin up, eyes like blue glass on fire with contempt, she drew the sheet around her. 'We made a deal in which I give you sex for six weeks until I can give you back your precious money. Show a bit of your so-called honour by keeping to that deal!'

With that she turned and strode off to the bathroom, needing to escape—needing some respite from Leo Christakis and his long, sexy body stretched out in that chair by the bed. So he'd pulled a robe on—what difference did that make? She could still see him naked, still visualise every honed muscle and bone, each single inch of his taut, bronzed flesh! And she could still feel the power of his kisses and the weight of him on top of her and the...

'You were innocent,' he fed after her.

Was he talking about her sexual innocence or her being innocent of all of the other rotten charges he had laid against her? Did she care? No.

'Stick to your first impression of me,' she flung at him over her shoulder. 'Your instincts were working better then!'

On that scathing slice, she slammed into the bathroom.

Leo grimaced into his glass. His first impression of Natasha Moyles had been deadly accurate, he acknowledged. It was only the stuff with Rico that had fouled up that impression.

He heard the shower running. He visualised her dropping the sheet and walking that smooth, curvy body into his custom-built wet room. The vision pushed him to his feet with the grim intention of giving into his nagging desires and going in there to join her. This war they were having was not over yet and would not be over until he won it.

Then something red caught the corner of his eye and he glanced down at the bed.

'Theos,' he breathed as his insides flipped into a near crippling squirm in recognition.

Proof that he had just taken his first virgin was staring him in the face like a splash of outrage.

Leo flexed his taut shoulders, glanced over at the closed door to the bathroom, then back at the bed. 'Damn,' he cursed, trying to visualise what she was going to feel like when she saw the evidence of her lost virginity, and added a few more oaths in much more satisfying Greek.

Instead of going to join her, he discarded his robe to snatch up his trousers and shirt and pulled them back on. He had no idea where Bernice kept the fresh bedlinen, but he was going to have to find out for himself because the hell if he was going to ask...

# CHAPTER SIX

WRAPPED in a spare bathrobe she'd found hanging behind the door, Natasha tugged in a deep breath, then opened the bathroom door and stepped out. Her heart was thumping. It had taken her ages to build up enough courage to leave the sanctuary of the bathroom and her muscles ached, she was so locked on the defensive, ready for her first glimpse of Leo sprawled in the chair by the bed.

It took a few moments for her to realise that she'd agonised over nothing because he wasn't even in the room. And the bed had been straightened so perfectly it looked as if it had never been used. Even her clothes had been picked up and neatly draped over the chair he had been sitting in.

Had Bernice come in here and tidied up after them? The very idea pushed a flush of mortified heat into her cheeks. Natasha dragged her eyes away from the bed and began scanning the room for her holdall, while wishing that someone had bothered to tell her that she was going to feel like this—all tense and edgy and horribly uncertain as to what happened after you jumped into bed with a man you hardly knew!

Then the bedroom door flew open and she spun to face it with a jerk. Half expecting to find Bernice or one of the maids

## The Harlequin Reader Service — Here's how it works:

walking in, she was really thrown into a wild flutter when it was Leo standing there.

He was dressed and she definitely wasn't. The way his eyes moved over her turned the flush of mortification into something else.

He swung the door shut behind him, then began striding towards her like some mighty warlord coming to claim his woman for a second round of mind-blowing sex and making her more uptight the closer he came. How could he wear that relaxed smile on his face as if everything in his world was absolutely perfect? Had he never felt awkward or nervous or just plain shy about anything?

Not this man, she concluded with a deep inner quiver when he pulled to a stop right in front of her. He gave off the kind of masculine vitality that made her fingers clutch the collar of the bathrobe close to her throat.

'Your hair is wet,' he observed, lifting a hand up to stroke it across the slicked back top of her head.

'Your state-of-the-art wet room has a w-will of its own,' she answered, still feeling the tingling shock she'd experienced when jets of water had hit her from every angle the moment she'd touched the start button in there.

'I'll find you a hairdryer,' he murmured as he moved his hand to stroke the hectic burn in her cheek. 'But in truth, I think you look adorable just as you are and if I thought you could take more of me right now I would be picking you up and taking you back to bed.'

Natasha shook his hand away. 'I wouldn't let you.'

'Maybe,' he goaded softly, 'you would find yourself with little choice?'

Natasha's startled gaze clashed with his smiling dark eyes. 'You would make me, you mean?'

'Seduce you into changing your mind, beautiful one,' he corrected, then lowered his head to steal a kiss.

And it wasn't just a quick steal. He let his lips linger long enough to extract a response from her before he drew back again.

'Fortunately for you, right now I am starving for real food,' he mocked her smitten expression. 'Find yourself something comfortable to put on while I shower, then we will go and eat.'

With that he strode into the bathroom. Arrogant—arrogant—*arrogant!* Natasha thought as she wiped the taste of his mouth from her lips.

Thoroughly out of sorts with herself for being so susceptible to him, she hunted down her holdall and used up some of her irritation by hauling it up onto the bed and yanking open the zip. For the next few seconds she just stood looking down into the bag with absolutely no clue whatsoever as to what the heck she had packed inside it. She only had this very vague memory of grabbing clothes at random, then dropping them into the bag. Tense fingers clutching the gaping robe to her throat again, she let the other hand rummage inside the bag and pulled out an old pair of jeans and a pale green T-shirt.

Great, she thought as she discarded those two unappealing garments onto the bed. A pair of ordinary briefs—not a thong, thank goodness—appeared next, and she tossed those onto the bed, too. She found another suit styled like the pale blue suit she'd been wearing all day, only this one was in a dull cream colour that made her frown because she could not imagine herself buying it, never mind wearing such an awful shade against her fair skin. Yet she must have bought it or it wouldn't be here.

Or perhaps this new Natasha—the one clutching a robe to her throat after losing her virginity to an arrogant Greek—had developed different tastes. She certainly felt different, kind of aching and alive in intimate places and so aware of her own body it started to tingle even as she thought about it.

No make-up, she discovered. She'd forgotten to pack her make-up bag or even a brush or comb. A couple of boring skirts appeared from the bag, followed by a couple of really boring tops. Frowning now with an itchy sense of dissatisfaction that irritated her all the more simply because she was feeling it, she finally unearthed a floaty black skirt made of the kind of fabric that didn't crease when she pulled it free of the bag. A black silk crocheted top appeared next, which was going to have to go with the skirt whether she liked it or not since she did not seem to have anything else like it in the bag.

Only one spare pair of shoes—and *no* spare bra! she discovered. Sighing heavily, she turned towards the chair where her other clothes were neatly folded, and was about to walk over there to recover her white bra—when Leo strode out of the bathroom.

It was as if she'd been thrown into an instant freeze the way she stood there between the bed and the chair, pinned to the polished wood floor while her busy mind full of what to wear came to a sudden halt.

Other than for the towel he had slung low around his lean waist, he was naked. Beads of water clung to the dark hairs on his chest. Her heart began to race as her eyes dropped lower, over the taut golden brown muscles encasing his stomach that shone warm and glossy and sinewy tight. The towel covered him from narrow hips and long powerful thighs to his knees, and the strength she could see structuring his calf muscles held her totally, utterly breath-shot as she felt the undiluted wash of what true desire really meant suffuse heat into each fine layer of her skin.

Oh, dear God, I want him badly, she acknowledged as those legs came to a sudden standstill and brought her eyes fluttering up to clash with his. It was like being suffocated, she likened dizzily, because she knew by the way he narrowed his eyes that he was reading her responses to him.

'I've forgotten to pack any m-make-up.' The words jumped from her in a panic-stricken leap.

He continued to stand there for a few more seconds just studying her, then he started walking again. 'You will not need make-up for dinner here alone with me,' he responded evenly.

Natasha pulled her eyes away from him to glance at the scramble of clothes she'd thrown onto the bed. 'I don't even have anything here fit to wear for dinner,' she said, trying desperately to sound as calm as he had when calm was the last thing she was feeling.

He came to a stop beside her. 'Wear the cream thing,' he suggested with only the vaguest hint of distaste showing in his voice.

It was enough. Natasha shook her head. 'I hate it.'

Beginning to frown now, he turned to look down at her. 'Natasha, what—'

'W-what are you going to wear?' she heard herself blurt out, then grabbed in a tense breath because—in all her life she had never asked a man such a gauche, stupid question! And his frown was darkening by the second. She could actually *feel* him mulling over what to say next! She wanted to call back her silly question. She *wished* she weren't even here!

She turned to face him. 'Listen Leo, I…'

Then it came—his shockingly unexpected answer to her problem: he dropped the towel from around his waist. 'Let's wear nothing,' he said.

The sheer outrageousness of the gesture completely robbed Natasha of speech. Heat flowed through her body, soaking her groin like hot pins and needles before spreading everywhere else. She tried to breathe. She tried to swallow. She tried to stop staring at him but she couldn't. She tried to back off when he reached across the gap between them, but her legs had turned to liquid and were refusing to move.

He reached for the hand she was using to clutch the bathrobe to her throat and gently prized her fingers free.

'Leo, no…' She mouthed the husky protest with her heart clattering wildly against her ribs because she knew what was coming next.

'Leo—yes,' he interpreted softly.

Two seconds later the bathrobe fell to the floor at her feet and his hands were taking its place. Freshly showered skin met with freshly showered skin and her naked breasts swelled and peaked. Her shaken gasp was captured by the sensual crush of his mouth and her troubled world tilted right out of kilter as the whole sexual merry-go-round spun off again. She didn't even want to stop it, she just threw herself into the dizzying pleasure of the kiss with her hands clutching at his solid biceps and her hips swaying closer to the burgeoning evidence of his desire and its formidable promise. Within seconds she was a quivering mass of nerve-endings, moving against him and kissing him back, her heart racing, her breathing reduced to fevered little tugs at oxygen filled with his intoxicating clean scent.

The sound of the bedroom door being thrown open with enough force to send it slamming back into something solid almost blew the top off her head. She flicked her eyes open. Leo was already lifting up his head. Way too dazed to think for herself, Natasha watched him shift the burning darkness of his eyes away from her to look towards the bedroom door, then copied him to look in that direction, too.

A woman stood there. A tall, reed-slender, staggeringly beautiful woman, wearing a dramatically short and slinky red satin dress. Her flashing black eyes were fixed on Leo, her exquisite face turning perfectly white.

'Gianna,' he greeted smoothly. 'Nice of you to drop in, but, as you can see, we are busy....'

As cool as that, he turned Natasha into a block of ice as his wife—his *ex*-wife—threw herself into a rage of shrill spitting Greek. Leo said absolutely nothing while the tirade poured out. His heart wasn't thundering. His breathing was steady. He just stood holding Natasha close as if trying to shield her nakedness with his own naked length, and let the other woman screech herself out.

It was awful. Natasha wished she could just sink into a hole in the ground. It was so humiliatingly obvious that Gianna felt she had a right to yell at Leo like this or why would she do it? Likening this situation to the one she'd witnessed between Cindy and Rico made her shiver in shame.

Feeling her shiver, Leo flicked a glance at her, then frowned as with a smooth grace he bent and scooped up the robe she had been wearing and draped it around her shoulders. 'Shut up now, Gianna,' he commanded grimly. 'You sound like a shrieking cat.'

To Natasha's surprise the shouting stopped. 'You were supposed to be at Boschetto's tonight,' Gianna switched to condemning English. 'I waited and waited for you to arrive and I felt the fool when you did not turn up!'

'I made no arrangement to meet up with you,' Leo said, bending a second time to pick up his towel, which wrapped back around his hips. 'So if you made a fool of yourself, you did it of your own volition.'

'You were expected—'

'Not by you,' Leo stated. 'Here, let me help you...'

Trying to push her arms into the robe sleeves, Natasha found Leo taking over the task, but, 'I'll do it myself,' she breathed tautly, and pushed his hands away.

She couldn't look at him—did not want to look at his ex-wife. Embarrassment was crawling around her insides and she felt so humiliated she was trembling with it.

Speaking earned Natasha Gianna's attention; she felt the other woman scythe a skin-peeling look over her. 'So you like them short and fat now?' she said to Leo.

Fat? Natasha burned up inside with indignation, huddling her size-ten figure into the all-encompassing bathrobe.

'Much better than a rake-thin whore with a sluttish heart,' Leo responded, reaching out to stroke one of his hands down Natasha's burning cheek as if in an apology for his witch of an ex-wife's insult. 'Now behave, Gianna, or I will have Rasmus throw you out of here. In fact,' he then drawled curiously, 'I will be very interested to hear how you got in here at all?'

Daring a glance at the other woman, Natasha saw that she was standing there with her slender arms folded across her slender ribs. She had to be six feet tall and the way she'd been poured into that red satin dress said everything there was to say about the differences between the two of them.

No wonder she still claimed super-model status, she concluded, flicking her eyes up to Gianna's fabulous bone-structure to see that her almond-shaped, Latin black eyes were gleaming defiance at Leo, her lush red mouth set in a provoking pout.

Leo released a soft, very cynical laugh as if he understood exactly what the look was conveying.

'So, who is she?' Gianna flicked another snide look at Natasha. 'Yet another attempt you make to find a substitute for me?'

Natasha flinched. Leo drew her back into his arms again and ignored her when she tried to pull back. 'Never in a thousand years could anyone substitute you, my sweet-tongued angel,' he mocked dryly. Then he looked down at Natasha and, with the silken tone of a man about to rock her world off its axis, 'In the form of a heartfelt apology to you, *agape mou,*' he murmured soft to Natasha, 'I must introduce you to Gianna, my ex-wife.'

'I am your ex-nothing!' Gianna erupted.

'Gianna.' He spoke right across the shrill protest. 'Nothing in this world has ever given me greater pleasure than to introduce you to Natasha, my very beautiful *future* wife.'

As a cool, slick way of dropping a bombshell, it was truly impressive. Staring up at his totally implacable face, Natasha almost fell backwards in shock.

The beautiful Gianna turned deathly white. 'No,' she whispered.

'You wish,' Leo responded.

'But you love *me!*' Gianna cried out in pained anguish.

'Once upon a time you were worth loving, Gianna. Now…?' He gave a shrug that said the rest, then apparently committed the ultimate sin in Gianna's eyes and leant down to capture Natasha's shock-parted lips with a kiss.

Without any warning it was about to happen, fresh pandemonium broke out with a keening wail that spliced up the atmosphere, then Gianna was coming at Natasha like a woman with murder in mind. Natasha jumped like a terrified rabbit. Leo spat out a curse and stepped right in front of her, taking the brunt of Gianna's fury upon himself.

It was horrible, the whole thing. Natasha could only stand there behind him, shocked into shaking while Leo contained his ex-wife's wrists to stop her long nails from clawing his face.

Then he bit out a terse, 'Excuse us…' to Natasha, and he was manhandling the screaming woman out of the bedroom.

The door thudded shut in his wake. Natasha found that her legs couldn't hold her up a moment longer and she sank in a whooshing loss of energy down onto the edge of the bed.

Beyond the door, Rasmus was just stepping out of the lift.

Leo sent him a glancing blow of a look and his security chief paled. 'I'm sorry, Leo,' he jerked out. 'I don't know—'

'Get her out of here,' Leo gritted. 'Take her home and sober her up.'

Gianna had stopped fighting and screeching now and was sobbing into his chest and clinging instead. Disgust flayed Leo's insides when it took the controlled strength of both men to transfer her from himself to Rasmus and get her into the lift.

'I don't know how she got in here,' Rasmus said helplessly.

'But you will do,' Leo lanced out. 'Then see to it that who-ever it was on your staff she laid in return for the favour is gone from here,' he instructed, then stabbed the button that shut the lift doors.

Alone in the hallway, he spun round in a full circle, then grabbed the back of his neck. Anger was pumping away inside him, contempt—repugnance. Having taken a telephone call from Gianna when he first arrived here, he'd told her that she had to get the hell off his back!

Her barging in here had been deliberate. Even the angry shrieking had been a put-up job. And the fact that she would not think twice about seducing one of his staff to get what she wanted was just another side to her twisted personality that filled him with disgust!

'*Theos*,' he muttered, long legs driving him through the apartment and pulling him to a halt outside the closed bed-room door, the knowledge that he'd lost the towel again having no effect on him at all.

He wasn't stupid. He knew that Gianna's nicely timed in-terruption had been a set-up, just as he knew the comparison Natasha had drawn from the moment it all kicked off.

Rico with her sister.

A curse ripped from him, followed by another. He paced out the width of the hall trying to clamp down on the anger still erupting inside him because—how the hell did he explain a sex-obsessed feline like Gianna, who only functioned this side of sane while she knew that he was always going to be around to help pick her up when she fell apart?

You didn't explain it. It was too damn complicated, he recognised as he took in a grim breath of air, then threw open the bedroom door.

Natasha was back in the blue suit, and she was stuffing her things back into her bag.

'Don't you pull a hysterical scene on me,' he rasped, closing the door with a barely controlled thud.

His voice sent a quiver down Natasha's tense spinal cord. 'I'm not hysterical,' she responded quietly.

'Then *what* do you call the way you are packing that bag?'

The searing thrust of his anger shocked even Leo as Natasha swung round to stare at him. Miss Cold and Prim was back with a vengeance, Leo saw, and she was stirring him up like...

She saw *it* happen, and lifted a pair of frosty blue eyes to his. 'Is that response due to her by any chance?' And her voice dripped disdain.

*Hell,* Leo cursed. 'Sorry,' he muttered, not sure exactly what it was he was apologising for—the snarling way he had spoken to her or his uncontrolled...

She spun her back to him again. Snapping his lips together, he strode over to the bank of glossy white wardrobes and tugged open one of the doors. A second later he was pulling a pair of jeans up his legs.

'She's mad,' he muttered.

'Enter the beautiful mad wife—exit the short, fat other woman.' Natasha pushed a pair of shoes into the bag.

'*Ex*-wife,' he corrected, tugging his zip up.

'Try telling her that.'

'I do tell her—constantly. As you saw for yourself, she does not listen—and you are not going anywhere, Natasha, so you can stop packing that bag.'

Straightening up, Natasha meant to spear him with another crushing look, only to find herself lose touch with what they were saying when she saw him standing there with his long legs encased in faded denim and looking like a whole new kind of man. Her heart gave a telling stuttering thud. Her breathing faltered. He was so blatantly, beautifully masculine it took a fight to drag her covetous mind back on track.

'S-so you thought you might as well make her listen by hitting her with that lie about a future wife?'

A frown darkened his lean features and made the bump on his nose stand out. 'It was not a lie, Natasha,' he declared like a warning.

'Oh, yes, it was,' she countered that. 'I wouldn't marry you if my life depended on it.'

'You mean, you are here merely to use me for sex?'

The sardonic quip was out before Leo could stop it.

'Substitute!' she tossed right back at him like the hot sting from a whip. 'And not even that again,' she added, yanking her eyes away from him altogether and zipping up the hastily packed bag with enough violence to threaten the teeth on the zip.

Easing his shoulders back against the wardrobe door, Leo folded his arms across his hair-roughened chest. 'So I was a tacky one-night substitute, then,' he prodded.

'Very tacky.' Pressing her lips together, she nodded in confirmation, then parted her lips to add bitterly, 'God save me from the super-rich class. Everything they do is so tacky it constantly makes me want to be sick.'

'Was that aimed at me, Gianna or Rico?'

'All three,' she said, frowning as she sent her eyes hunting the room for her purse. She couldn't see it anywhere and she couldn't recall when she had last had it in her hand.

'Lost something valuable?' his hatefully smooth voice questioned. 'Like your virginity, perhaps?'

It was as good as a hard slap in the face. Natasha tugged in a hot breath. 'I've just remembered why I dislike you so much.'

His wide shoulders gave a deeply bronzed shrug against the white wardrobe. He looked like some brooding dark male model posing for one of the big fashion magazines, Natasha thought, feebly aware that her eyes refused to stay away from him for more than ten seconds before they dragged themselves back again because he was so bone-tinglingly good to look at. Sexuality oozed out of every exposed manly pore and those jeans should be X-rated. How had she ever thought that he was nothing to look at next to Rico? If Rico dared to stride in here right now and stand next to this man, Natasha knew she wouldn't even see him. Leo won hands down in each single aspect of his dominant masculine make-up—even the bump in his nose yelled sexually exciting unreconstructed male at her!

*Oh, what's happening to me?* On that helplessly bewildered inward groan, she yanked her eyes away from him— yet again—and *made* them search the room for her purse! In less than a day it felt as if everything she'd ever held firm about herself had been corkscrewed out of her then mixed around violently before being shoved back inside her to form this entirely new perspective on everything!

And the way he was standing there looking at her with his eyes thoughtfully narrowed just wasn't right, either—as if he was considering striding over here and *showing* her the tough way in which this new order of things worked.

A sensation Natasha just did not want to feel spread itself right down her front. Tense upper lip quivering—she just *had* to get out of here.

'Have you seen my purse?'

'What do you need it for?'

Straightening her tense shoulders, she said, 'I'm ready to leave now.'

'By what form of transport?'

'Taxi!' she spat out.

'You have the Euros to pay for a taxi?' her cool tormentor quizzed. 'And a mobile phone handy to call one up? Do you speak any Greek, *agape mou*? Do you even know this address so you can tell the taxi driver where to come to collect you?'

He was deliberately beating her up with blunt logic. 'Y-you have my mobile phone,' she reminded him, hating that revealing quiver in her voice.

He responded to that with yet another of those irritatingly expressive shrugs against the glossy white wardrobe door. 'I must have mislaid it, as you have your purse.'

Deciding the only way to deal with the infuriatingly impossible brute was to ignore him, Natasha started hunting the bedroom.

While Leo watched her do it, his narrowed gaze ran over the way she looked all neat and tidy in every which way she could be—except for the wet hair which lay in a heavy silk pelt down her back. A man could not find a bigger contrast between Natasha's cool dignity and Gianna's reckless abandon, Leo observed grimly. Where Gianna clung to him like a weeping vine, this aggravating woman was preparing to walk out on him!

'Tell me, Natasha,' he asked grimly, 'why are you so eager to leave when only ten minutes ago you were ready to fall back into bed with me?'

'Your wife got in here somehow,' she muttered, checking beneath one of the cushions on the chair to see if her purse had slid behind it.

'Ex-wife—and...?'

'Maybe her claim on you has some justification,' Natasha said with a shrug.

'Like…?' he prompted, and there was no hint whatsoever left of the provoking mockery with which he had started this conversation. He was deadly curious to hear where she was going with this.

'The way you run your life is your own business.' Chickening out at the last second from stating outright the real question that was beating a hole in her head, she gave up on the chair and tossed the cushion back onto it.

But—did he still sleep with his ex-wife when he felt like it? Did Gianna have a genuine right to her grievances when she'd barged in on them as she had? If so, then it made him no better than Rico in the way that he treated women!

Tacky, as she'd already said. She returned to her search with his brooding silence twitching at her nerve-ends as she moved about the room.

'I do not have a relationship with my ex-wife,' he spoke finally. 'I do not sleep with her and I have no wish to sleep with her, though Gianna prefers to tell herself I will change my mind if she pushes long and hard enough… In case you did not notice,' he continued as Natasha turned to look him, 'Gianna is not quite—stable.'

It was the polite way to call it, but Natasha could see by the flick of a muscle at the corner of his mouth that he was holding back from voicing his real thoughts about Gianna's mental health. And what did she do? She stood here eating up every single word like some lovelorn teenager in need of his reassurance.

'In some ways I still feel responsible for her because she *was* my wife and I *did* care for her once—until she pressed the self-destruct button on our marriage for reasons not up for discussion here.' And the tough way he said that warned her not to try to push him on it. 'I apologise that she barged in here and embarrassed you,' he expressed curtly. 'I apologise that she found a way to enter this property at all!' A fresh burst of anger straightened him away from the wardrobe. 'But that's it—that is as far as I am prepared to go to make you feel better about the situation, Natasha. So stop behaving like a tragic bride on her wedding night and take the damn jacket off before *I* take it off!'

'W-what—?' Not quite making the cross-over from his grim explanation about Gianna to the sudden attack on herself, Natasha blinked at him.

Which seemed to infuriate him all the more. 'While you stand here playing the poor, abused victim, you seem to have conveniently forgotten about the money you stole from me!'

The money.

Natasha tensed up, then froze as if he'd reached out and hit her. Leo smothered a filthy curse because her hesitation told him that she *had* forgotten all about the money. Though the curse was aimed at himself for reminding her about it when he would have preferred it to remain forgotten about! Now she was looking so pale and appalled he grimly wondered if she was going to pass out on him.

A tensely gritted sigh had him striding over to her. Lips pinned together, he reached out and began unbuttoning her jacket with tight movements that bore no resemblance whatsoever to the other times he had taken it upon himself to do this.

She didn't even put up a fight, but just stood there like a waxen dummy and let him strip the garment from her body, which only helped to infuriate him all the more! With the muscles across his shoulders bunching, he tossed the jacket aside, then turned to walk back across the room to the wardrobes. Hunting out a white T-shirt, he dragged it on over his head.

When he turned back to Natasha, he found her still standing where he'd left her, giving a good impression of a perfectly pale ghost.

*Theos*, he thought, wondering why seeing her looking so beaten was making his senses nag the hell out of him to just go over there and apologise yet again—for being such a brute.

'Dinner,' he said, taking another option, keeping up the tough tone of voice because—well, she was a cheating thief even if he wanted to forget that she was!

At last she moved—or her pale lips did. 'I'm not hungry—'

'You are eating,' he stated. 'You have had nothing since you threw up in my London basement.'

And reminding her of that was Leo Christakis well and truly back as the blunt-speaking insensitive brute, Natasha noted.

Even in the T-shirt and chinos.

And his feet bare...

She felt like crying again, though why the sight of his long, bronzed bare feet moving him so gracefully across the room to the door made her want to do that Natasha did not have a clue, but suddenly she just wanted to sit in a huddle in a very dark corner somewhere and...

He pulled the bedroom door open, then stood there pointedly waiting for her to join him. Head lowered, she went because there was no point in continuing to argue with him when all he had to do was to mention the money to devastate her every line of defence.

Hard, tough, unforgivably ruthless, she reminded herself, wondering how she had allowed herself to forget those things about him while she had been giving him free use of her body—as a part of their *deal*.

She didn't look at him as she walked past him and out into the hallway. She kept her head lowered when he stepped in front of her to lead the way through the apartment and into a room lit by flickering candle-light and another glass wall.

Bernice was there, arranging the last pieces of cutlery on a white linen tablecloth intimately set for two. Candles flickered. Beyond the table stood the night view of Athens, making the most romantic backdrop any woman could wish for.

Any romantically hopeful woman, that was.

Friction stung the atmosphere and the housekeeper smiled and said something in Greek to Leo. He replied in the same language as he held out a chair for Natasha to use. After that there was no privacy to speak of anything personal because a maid arrived to serve them. Natasha had a feeling Leo had arranged it that way so he didn't get into yet another dogfight with her, but the tension between them made it almost impossible to swallow anything, though she did try to eat. When she couldn't manage to swallow another beautifully presented morsel, she stared at the view beyond the glass window, or down at the leftover food on her plate, or at the crisp white wine he had poured into the glass she was fingering without drinking—anywhere so long as it wasn't at him.

Then he shattered it. Without any hint at all that one swift glance from his eyes had sent the maid disappearing out of the room, Leo suddenly leant forwards and stretched a hand out across the table and brazenly cupped her left breast.

'I knew it,' he husked. 'You are wearing no bra, you provoking witch.'

Pleasure senses went into overdrive. Natasha shot like a sizzling firework rocket to her feet. He rose up more slowly, face taut, his dark eyes flickering gold in the candle-light.

'Don't ever touch me like that without my permission again,' she shook out in a pressured whisper, then she turned to stumble around her chair and made a blind dash out of the room.

The lift stood there with its doors conveniently open. Natasha did not even have to think about it as she dashed inside and sent the lift sweeping down to the ground floor. Outside in the garden the thick, humid air was filled with the scent of oranges. Soft lighting drew her down winding pathways between carefully nurtured shrubs and beneath the orange laden trees. She didn't know where she was heading for, all she did know was that she needed to find that dark corner she could huddle in so she could finally—finally give in to the tears she'd held back too long.

She found it in the shape of a bench almost hidden beneath the dipping branches of a tree close to the high stuccoed wall that surrounded the whole property. Dropping down onto the bench, she pulled her knees up to her chin, leant her forehead on them, then let go and wept. She wept over everything. She just trawled it all out and took a good look at everything from the moment she'd opened the message on her mobile telephone that morning to the moment Leo had touched her breast across the dinner table—and she wept and she wept and she wept.

Leo leant against a trunk of the tree and listened. Inside he had never felt so bad in his life. The way he had been treating her all day had been nothing short of unforgivable. The way he'd made love to her when he'd known she should have been doing this instead was going to live on his conscience for a long time to come.

But the way he had reached across the dinner table and touched her just now was, without question, the lowest point to which he had stooped.

And listening to her weep her soul into shreds was his deserved punishment. Except that he couldn't stand to listen to it any longer and, with a sigh, he levered away from the tree trunk and went to sit down beside her, then lifted her onto his lap.

She tried to fight him for a second or two, but he just murmured, 'Shh, sorry,' and held her close until she stopped fighting him and let the tears flow again.

When it was finally over and she quietened, he stood up

with her in his arms and took her back inside. He did it without saying a single word, ignoring the dozen or so security cameras he knew would have been trained on them from the moment Natasha ran outside.

She was asleep, he realised when he lay her down on the bed. With the care of a man dealing with something fragile, he slipped off her shoes and her skirt, then covered her with the sheets.

Straightening up again, he continued to stand there for a few seconds looking down at her, then he turned and walked out of the bedroom and into his custom-built office.

A minute later, 'Juno,' he greeted. 'My apologies for the lateness of the hour, but I have something I need you to do....'

## CHAPTER SEVEN

NATASHA drifted awake to soft daylight seeping in through the wall of curved glass and to instant recall that sent her head twisting round on her pillow to check out the other side of the bed.

The sudden pound her heart had taken up settled back to its normal pace when she discovered that she was alone, the only sign that she had shared the bed at all through the night revealed by the indent she could see in the other pillow and the way Leo had thrown back the sheets when he'd climbed out.

Then the whispering suggestion of a sound beyond the bedroom door told her what it was that had awoken her in the first place, and she was up, rolling off the bed and running for the bathroom, only becoming aware as she did so that she was still wearing the white top she'd spent most of the day yesterday in.

So he'd shown a bit of rare sensitivity by not stripping her naked, she acknowledged with absolutely no thought of gratitude stirring in her blood. Leo had taken her to pieces yesterday brick by brutal brick, so one small glimpse of humanity in him because he'd put her limp self to bed and had the grace to leave her with some dignity in place did not make her feel any better about him.

She stepped into the wet room, with her hair safely wrapped away inside a fluffy white towel, frowned and at the range of keypads and dials, trying to work out how she could take a shower without having to endure a thorough dousing at the same time. Leo Christakis was one of life's takers, she decided. He saw an opportunity and went for it. He'd wanted her so he just moved in on her like a bulldozer and scooped her up.

Water jets suddenly hit her from all angles, making mockery of the buttons she'd pushed to stop them from doing it. A gasping breath shot from her as the jets stung her flesh. The sensation was so acute it made her look down at her body, half expecting to see that it had altered physically somehow, but all she saw was her normal curvy shape with its pale skin, full breasts and rounded hips with a soft cluster of dusky curls shaping the junction with her thighs.

But she had changed inside where it really mattered, Natasha accepted. She'd become a woman in a single day. One stripped of her silly daydreams about love and romance, then made to face cold reality—that you didn't need love or romance to fall headlong into pleasures of the flesh.

You didn't need anything but the desire to reach out and take it when it was right there in front of you to take.

Rico was like that. So was her sister, Cindy. They saw, they desired, so they took. It was there to take, so why not? Now she might as well accept that she'd joined the ranks of takers because she could stand here letting the shower jets inflict their torture on her and try to convince herself that she'd been blackmailed and bullied into Leo's bed, but it was never going to be the truth.

She'd wanted, she'd let him see it, Leo had taken, now it was done. What a fabulous introduction to the reality of life.

Bernice was walking in from the terrace when Natasha came out of the bathroom back in the bathrobe once again. Feeling a hot wave of shyness wash over her, Natasha felt like diving back into the bathroom and hiding there until the housekeeper had gone but it was already too late.

Bernice had seen her. 'Kalemera, thespinis,' the housekeeper greeted with a smile. 'It is a beautiful day to eat breakfast outside, is it not?'

'Perfect.' Natasha managed a return smile, 'Thank you, Bernice,' she added politely.

Walking towards the wall of glass as Bernice left the room, she pushed her hands into the deep pockets of her robe and stepped out into a crystal-clear morning bathed in sunlight and the inviting aroma of hot coffee and toast. By the sudden growl her stomach gave she was hungry, Natasha realised, which shouldn't surprise her when she'd barely eaten anything the day—

Her mind and her feet pulled to a sudden standstill. For some crazy reason she just had not expected to find Leo out here seated at the table set for breakfast. However, there he sat, calmly reading a newspaper with a cup of hot coffee hovering close to his mouth.

Her soft gasp of surprise brought his eyes up from the newspaper, his heavy eyelashes folding back from liquid-dark irises that swamped her in heated awareness as they stroked up the length of her from bare toes to the tangling tumble of her unbrushed hair.

'Kalemera,' he murmured softly, and he rose to his feet.

It was like being hit head on by all the things she had not allowed herself to think about since she'd woken up this morning—the man in the flesh. Even though he was wearing a conventional business suit a warm tug of remembered intimacy made itself felt between her thighs. She found her eyes doing much the same thing as his eyes had done, feathering up the length of his long legs encased in smooth-as-silk iron-grey fabric, then his torso covered by a pale blue shirt and dark tie. By the time she reached his clean-shaven face with its too-compellingly, strong golden features, she was blushing and annoyed enough by it to push up her chin.

'Good morning,' she returned in cool English.

A half-smile clipped at the corners of his mouth. 'You slept well, I trust?'

He met her challenge with mockery.

'Yes, thank you.' Natasha kept with cool.

Pulling her eyes off him, she dug her hands deeper into her robe pockets, curled them into tense fists, then made herself walk towards the table and slip into the chair opposite him, expecting Leo to return to his seat, but he didn't.

'Bernice was unsure what you preferred to eat for breakfast so she has provided a selection.' A long, lean hand indicated another table standing to one side of the terrace, which was spread with covered dishes. 'Tell me what you would like and I'll get it for you.'

Glancing at it, then away again, 'Thank you, I'm fine with just toast.'

'Juice?' he offered.

A small hesitation, then she nodded. 'Please.'

He went to pour the juice from the jug set on the other table. You couldn't get a more pleasantly generated scene of calm domesticity if you tried, Natasha noted—though there was nothing domesticated in the way her eyes had to follow him or the way they soaked in every inch of his powerful lean frame like greedy traitors.

Looking away quickly when he turned around, she pretended an interest in the daytime view of Athens glistening in a hazy sunlight. Then one of his hands appeared in front of her to set down the glass of juice. Ice chinked against freshly squeezed oranges. He did not move away and another of those hesitations erupted between them sending out vibrating signals Natasha just did not want to read. And he was standing so close she could smell the clean, tangy scent of him, could *feel* the sheer masculine force of his sexuality that to her buzzing mind was barely leashed.

Then he brought his other hand around her to settle a rack of toast next to the glass of juice.

'Thank you,' she murmured.

'My pleasure,' he drawled—and he moved away to return to his seat, leaving Natasha to pull in a breath she had not been aware she had been holding on to.

He picked up his coffee cup and his newspaper.

Tugging her hands out of her pockets, she picked up the glass and sipped the juice. The sun beat down on the gardens below them while the overhang from the roof suspended above the terrace kept them in much pleasanter shade.

She was about to help herself to a slice of toast when she saw her mobile telephone lying on the table and her fingers stilled in midair.

'Bernice found it in my jacket pocket. I had forgotten I had it.' He might give the appearance of being engrossed in his newspaper, but he clearly was not.

Having to work to stop yet another polite thank-you from developing, Natasha pressed her lips together and nodded, then picked the phone up, her fingers stroking the shiny black casing for a few seconds before she flipped the phone open and looked at the screen.

It filled up with voice and text messages from Rico or Cindy. Aware that Leo was watching her, aware of the silence thickening between the two of them, she began to delete each message in turn, gaining a cold kind of pleasure from watching each one disappear from the screen. As the final one disappeared she flipped the phone shut and placed it back on the table before reaching for the slice of toast.

'I need to shop for some clothes,' she said coolly.

Leo said nothing, though Natasha could feel his desire to say *something* about the way she had wiped her phone clean. Had *he* read her messages? Had he expected to find a volley of instructions from Rico instructing her on how to sneak away from here so she could hole up with him somewhere until the six weeks were up and they could get at their stolen stash?

What Leo did do was to reach inside his jacket pocket and come out with a soft leather wallet. 'I will arrange an account for you with my bank,' he said evenly, 'but for now…'

A thick wad of paper money landed on the table next to her phone. Cringing inside, Natasha just stared at it.

'Buy anything you want,' he invited casually. 'Rasmus will drive you into Athens—'

'I don't need a driver,' she whispered tautly. 'I can find my way to the shops by myself.'

'Rasmus will not be there merely to play chauffeur,' his smooth voice returned. 'He will escort you wherever you go while you are here.'

'For what purpose?' Natasha forced herself to look at him—forced herself to keep silent about the phone and the hateful money he'd tossed down next to it. 'To guard me in case I decide to run out on you? Well, I won't run,' she stated stiffly. 'I don't want to be thrown into jail if I get caught.'

'In that case think of Rasmus as protection,' he suggested.

'Which I need because…?'

The attractive black arc of his eyebrows lifted upwards. 'Because it is a necessary evil in this day and age?' he offered.

'For you perhaps.'

'You are an intimate part of me now, which means you must learn to take the bad with the good.'

So where was the good in being his woman? she wondered

furiously. 'People would have to know I'm with you to make a bodyguard necessary for me.'

'But they will know—from tonight,' he countered, calmly folding his newspaper on that earth-rocking announcement. 'We will be dining out with some friends of mine. So while you are shopping buy a dress—something befitting a black-tie event. Something—pretty.'

Pretty? 'I don't do pretty.' Reaching for the pot of marmalade, Natasha began spreading it liberally on the toast.

'Something—colourful, then to—complement your figure.'

'I am not—' the knife worked faster '—going to dress up like some floozy just to help you prove a point to your awful ex-wife!'

'Why? Don't you believe you have the power to compete?'

The challenge hit Natasha blindside, and she felt her breath stick in her throat.

'It seems to me, Natasha, that you're too easily intimidated by conceited bullies like your selfish sister and my ex-wife,' he went on grimly. 'Woman like them can pick a shrinking violet like you out from a hundred feet away as an easy target. But what really gets to me is that you let them. Grow up, *agape mou*,' he advised as he climbed to his feet. 'Toughen up. You are with me now and I have a reputation for high standards in my choice of women.'

Tense as piano wire now, 'Your standard must have slipped when you married Gianna, then,' she hit back at him.

To her further fury he just uttered a dry husky laugh! 'We are all allowed one mistake. Rico was your mistake, Gianna was mine, so now we are quits.'

With no quick answer ready to offset that one, 'Why don't you just go and do—whatever it is you do and leave me alone?' she muttered, and picked up her slice of toast to bite into it.

The next thing she knew he'd moved around the table and was swooping down to capture her marmalade sticky mouth.

'Mmm, nice,' he murmured as he drew away again. 'I think we will try that again…'

Dipping a fingertip into the marmalade pot, he smeared it across the hot cushion of her bottom lip, then bent his dark head to lick the marmalade off. Like a captivated cat Natasha couldn't stop the pink tip of her own tongue from tracing her lip the moment he withdrew again.

'Yes,' he said softly, and she was drowning in a completely new kind of sensual foreplay that made her want to squirm where she sat.

Then he was straightening up to his full height and moving away from her towards the wall of glass with the smooth stride of an arrogantly self-confident male, leaving the rich, low sound of his amused laughter behind in his wake.

'You forgot to add yourself to the list of bullies in my life!' she threw after him, angrily snatching up a napkin to rub the residue of sticky marmalade from her mouth.

'But Miss Cool and Prim quickly slipped her chains, did she not? Think about it, Natasha.'

The glass slid open to allow him to stride through. Natasha stared after him until she couldn't see him any longer and sizzled and simmered—because she knew he was right. She had lost her cool the moment he'd touched her. It just wasn't fair that he could affect her that easily—it wasn't!

Her eyes went back to the wad of money still lying on the table where he'd tossed it down beside her phone. She was not so dumb that she hadn't recognised his criticism of her clothes and her uncompetitive nature for the challenge it was, but it had hurt to hear him say it in that disparaging tone he'd used.

Mr Blunt, she mocked dully, and felt the hurt tremor attack her poor, abused bottom lip.

Her mobile phone started ringing as she sat in the isolated luxury of one of Leo's limousines. Opening her purse—which

Bernice had also found for her this morning languishing on a table out on the terrace—Natasha plucked out her mobile phone and stared at the screen warily, expecting the caller to be Cindy or Rico, but it wasn't.

'How did you get my number?' she demanded.

'I stole it,' Leo confessed. 'Listen,' he then continued briskly, 'I have had an extra meeting dropped on me today so I will not be finished here in time to get back home and change before we go out. I have arranged with a friend of mine to kit you out with everything you might need in the way of clothes. Her name is Persephone Karides. Rasmus is transporting you to her salon right now. Don't turn stiff on her, *agape mou*,' he cautioned smoothly as if he just couldn't stop himself from criticising her! 'Trust her because she has more sense of style in her little fingertip than anyone else I know.'

Natasha drew in a hurt breath. 'You're very insulting,' she said as she breathed out again. 'Do you always have to think with your mouth?'

There was a silence—a short, sharp shock of one that rang in her ears and made her bottom lip quiver again. 'My apologies,' he murmured—earnestly. 'I did not intend what I said to sound like a criticism of you.'

'Well, it did.' Natasha flipped her phone shut and pushed it back in her bag. It rang again almost immediately but she ignored it.

'Oh, goodness me,' Persephone Karides gasped the moment she saw Natasha. 'When Leo told me you were different, I did not think he meant so fabulously different!'

Standing here in her miserable cream suit eyeing the eye-catching, raven-haired, tall, slender model-type standing a good six inches higher than herself—Natasha had to ask herself if Leo had primed Persephone Karides to say that.

'He's desperate I don't show him up by appearing in a sack, so he sent me to you,' she responded—stiffly.

'Are you joking?' Persephone Karides burst out laughing. 'Leo is much more concerned with his own comfort! He instructed me that he wants modest. He wants quietly elegant and refined. He does not want other men climbing over each other to get a better look at your front! I have not had as much fun in a long time as I did listening to a jealously possessive Leo Christakis, of all men, dictate how he wanted me to protect him!'

Natasha flushed at his intervention. Was he throwing down yet another challenge to her here or was Persephone Karides simply telling it as it was?

Whichever, the fact that he'd dared to give out such arrogant orders to the fashion stylist was enough to put the glinting light of defiance in her blue eyes.

Long hours later Rasmus pulled the car to a stop next to a fabulous-looking private yacht tied up against the harbour wall. Natasha gaped at it because the last thing she'd expected was to be dining in a restaurant situated on a luxury yacht.

'The boss owns it,' Rasmus told her as he shut off the car engine. 'The yacht used to belong to his father. When he decided to sell it, the boss objected. His father let him have the boat so long as he turned it into a profit-making enterprise.'

So he came up with the idea of turning the yacht into a restaurant? 'How old was he?' Natasha questioned curiously.

'Nineteen. He gave her a complete refit, then chartered her out and turned in a profit in his first year,' Rasmus said with unmistaken pride in his voice. 'Two years ago, when she was ready for another refit, he decided her sailing days were over and brought her here. Now she's one of the most exclusive restaurants in Athens.'

Here was a pretty horseshoe-shaped harbour tucked away

from the busy main port, Natasha saw when she climbed out of the car into the hot evening air, cooled by the gentle breeze coming in off the sea. The yacht itself had an old-world grandeur about it that revealed a sentimental side to Leo she would never have given him in a thousand years.

Or it reveals his money-making genius, the cynical side to her brain suggested to her as she walked up the gangway. She felt butterflies take flight in her stomach the closer she came to putting on show her day of defiance aided and abetted by an eager Persephone Karides.

Though the way she had allowed the moment to become so important to her came to lie like a weight across her chest when she saw him. He was leaning against a white painted bulkhead waiting for her. Natasha stilled as her spindle-heeled shoes settled onto the deck itself. He looked breath-shatteringly gorgeous in the conventional black dinner suit he was wearing with a black silk bow tie and a shimmering bright white shirt.

Uncertainty went to war against defiance as she waited for him to say something—show smug triumph because he had manipulated her to do what he wanted her to do or reveal his disapproval at the look she had achieved.

He took his own sweet time showing anything at all as he slid his hooded gaze over her from the top of her loose blonde hair tamed into heavy silk waves around her face and her bare shoulders, then took in the creamy, smooth thrust of her breasts cupped in a misty soft violet crêpe fabric held in place by two flimsy straps, which tied together at the back of her neck. The rest of the dress moulded every curving shape of her figure and finished modestly at her knees—though there was nothing remotely modest about the flirty little back kick pleat that gave her slender thighs length and a truly eye-popping—to Natasha anyway—sensual shape.

Sexy… She knew she looked sexy because Persephone had

told her she did and, as she'd learned during the long day in the Greek woman's care, Persephone did not mess around with empty compliments. 'Leo is going to kill me if you wear that,' she'd said.

And, true to Persephone's warning, Natasha saw that Leo was not happy. His growing frown teased her stomach muscles with a tingling surge of triumph. His mouth was flat, his eyes hidden beneath those disgustingly thick, ebony eyelashes. When he lifted a hand to run an absent finger along his bumpy nose, for some unaccountable reason she wanted to breathe out a victorious laugh.

Then she didn't want to laugh because he was lowering the hand and coming towards her, crossing the space separating them without uttering a single word. The expanse of creamy flesh she had on show began to prickle as he came closer, her wide-spaced, carefully made-up eyes with their eyelashes darkened and lengthened by a heavy lick of mascara trying their very best to appear cool. He came to a stop a few inches away, glanced down at her mouth so sensually shaped by a deep rose gloss, then dropped his gaze even lower, to the misty violet framework of the dress where it formed a perfect heart shape across the generous curves of her breasts.

By the time he lifted his eyes back to hers, Natasha felt as if she were standing on pins. She'd stopped breathing, was barely even thinking much beyond the sizzling clash their eyes had made. Then instinct kicked in and she lifted her chin in an outright challenge.

He slid his hands around her nipped-in waist, tugged her hard up against him, then stole her lipstick with a very hot, aggressive kiss.

'Move an inch from my side tonight and you will find

yourself floating in the water.' His eyes burned the threat into her as he drew away.

'It was you that told me to stop playing the shrinking violet,' she reminded him coolly.

Taking a small step back, he took his time looking her over once again. 'The colour of the dress is right anyway,' he observed finally.

Natasha pulled in a breath., 'Do you find it so totally impossible to say anything nice to me?'

She had a point, Leo acknowledged, but if she thought he had not noticed how pleased she was that she'd annoyed him, then—

'Come on,' he sighed, giving up because he'd got exactly what he'd asked for, and to discover only when it was too late that he no longer wanted it was his problem, not Natasha's. 'Let's find out if we can spend a whole evening together without embarking on yet another fight.'

Walking beside him with one of his long fingered hands a possessive clamp around her waist, Natasha wished she knew if it was triumph or annoyance that was sending sparking electrodes swimming in her blood. The moment they stepped inside the main salon she was immediately struggling with a different set of new conflicts when she found herself the instant centre of attention for twenty or so curious looks.

She moved a bit closer to Leo. Her hand slid up beneath his jacket to clutch tensely at his shirt against his fleshless waist. He liked it, she realised as she sensed a kind of quickening inside him as if his flesh had woken up to her presence. She went to snatch her hand back again, shocked that she'd even dared to put it there in the first place.

'Leave it where it is,' Leo instructed.

Her fingers quivered a little before they settled back against his shirt again. He responded with a delicate caress of her waist. Quickly the sensual charge that had been sparking between them from the moment they first kissed at his home in London was relaying its message again.

He began introducing her around his guests as 'Natasha', that was all, because to add the Moyles was bound to give rise to speculation about Rico, since half the people she was being introduced to were also on the wedding invitation list Rico's mother had emailed to her only last week.

And thinking about Rico did not make her feel comfortable about being here. It began to bother her that Leo had brought her into these people's midst at all. In fact, the more she thought about it, the more sure she became that, once these people found out the truth about exactly who she was, they were going to stop treating her with respect. At the moment they were only doing so because she was with Leo Christakis.

It also began to bother her that she needed to stick this close to Leo—touching, feeling his body warmth and his possessive arm across her back, his hand fixed like a clamp to her waist. Putting herself on show had never been her thing and it took only half an hour of being the centre of attention before she was certain she was never going to want to do it again.

Dinner took place in another salon, presided over by one of Athens's top chefs, she was reliably informed by a friend of Leo's seated opposite her. 'Leo likes only the best in everything,' Dion Angelis told her, grinning at the man in question who occupied the place next to Natasha.

Dion Angelis was about Leo's age and wore the same cloak of wealth about him—as all these people did. The beautiful creature sitting beside him was Marina, his very Greek wife.

Greek wives didn't speak to other men's lovers—at least not in this circle of people, Natasha had discovered tonight. And now she knew why as she watched Dion Angelis drift a lazy look over her with his eyelids lowered in a way she would have to be blind to miss what it meant.

Tensing slightly in her seat, Natasha flicked a glance at Marina who tried her best to hide her anger at her husband's blatant interest—but not before she had sent Natasha a scathing look of contempt. Then she slid her dark gaze to Leo.

'Leonadis...' it made Natasha start in surprise because she had not heard anyone call Leo that before '...Gianna expected you at Boschetto's last night. She was really quite upset when you failed to appear.'

Sitting further back into her chair, Natasha turned her expression blank. So even ex-wives rated higher than lovers, she gleaned from Marina's attempt to put her in her place.

'Gianna has already voiced her objection,' Leo returned smoothly. 'Dion, kindly remove your eyes from my future wife's breasts...'

As a softly spoken show-stopper it silenced a room full of chattering voices. The sophisticated Dion turned a dull shade of red. His wife snapped her lips together and turned her widening stare onto Natasha along with everyone else. Natasha was the only one to turn her shocked stare onto Leo while he, the cool, implacable devil, stared down at his wineglass and remained perfectly calm and relaxed with the kind of smile playing with his lips that turned Natasha's flesh to ice.

'Congratulations,' someone murmured, setting off a rippling effect of similar sentiments while Natasha continued to stare at Leo until he lifted his head and looked back at her, his steady, dark gaze silently challenging her to deny what he'd said.

It was on the tip of her tongue to do it. It was right there hovering on that tingling tip that she should just get it all over with and announce to everyone exactly who she was!

With an ease that belied the speed with which he did it and the strength that he used, Leo's hand caught hold of hers and squeezed. 'Don't,' he warned softly.

He was back to reading her mind again—back to playing it tough! Natasha turned to look at Marina, the light of fury like a crystal-blue haze she could barely manage to see through. 'Tacky, other people's relationships, don't you think?' she remarked with a wry smile that beat Leo's hands down in the chilly stakes. 'I can only hope that my marriage to Leo will come to a less volatile ending than his first marriage did and that I accept it with more—grace.'

With that she stood up, shaking inside now but knowing that she had made her point. She already knew about Gianna. She knew the ex-wife still chased her lost man. And she also knew that Leo had just said what he had because Marina's husband had been eyeing Natasha up and that Dion did it because other men's lovers were clearly fair game around here—which said what about Marina's place in her husband's life?

Leo also came to his feet, his hand still a crushing clamp around her fingers, which kept her pinned to his side. 'Excuse us,' he said dryly to their captive audience. 'It seems that Natasha and I need to find some privacy to discuss her desire to consign our marriage to the divorce courts before it has even begun.'

With that he turned and strode towards the exit, towing her behind him like some naughty child, while leaving a nervously uncertain shimmer of laughter to swim in their wake.

'You always planned to make that announcement, didn't you?' She leapt on the accusation the moment Rasmus closed them inside the car. 'It was the reason why you took me into their company, the reason why you sent me to Persephone to make sure I was suitably dressed for the part!'

'You chose your own style makeover, Natasha,' Leo imparted without a single hint of remorse for what he had just done. 'I recall warning Persephone that I wanted quietly elegant.'

The look she flicked him should have seared off a layer of his skin. 'Before or after you challenged me to put it all out on show?'

A muscle along his jaw flexed. 'I changed my mind about that.'

'Why?' she demanded.

Leo released an irritated sigh. 'Because I feel safer when you play it prim!'

The fact that he was actually admitting it was enough to stop Natasha's breath in her throat.

'Why does this surprise you?' he asked when he caught her expression. 'Your modest mystique was the first thing to attract me to you. Having come to know you a little better, I now realise that I prefer it if you remain mysterious—to everyone else but me.'

'That is just so arrogant I can't believe you even said it!'

All he offered was an indifferent shrug. 'Marina attacked you tonight because she believes you are merely my current lover. Now she knows that my intentions are honourable she will not dare to treat you like that again.'

'Until she finds out who I really am, then she will see the dangerous woman again—the kind that drops one brother to take up with the richer one!'

'Well, that puts Dion out of the frame,' Leo drawled with cool superiority. 'And as for Marina, she will make sure he keeps his wandering eyes to himself from now on.'

'I'm still not marrying you,' Natasha shook out, 'so it's up to you how you get out of the mess you made for yourself.'

Leo met that with silence. Natasha turned to look directly ahead and let the silence stretch. But she could feel his eyes on her, *feel* him trying to decide if she possessed enough determination against his relentless push to get her to agree to marry him, and she could feel the fizz in her insides—as if her newly awakened senses found it stimulating to be constantly sparring with him like this!

Leo was silent because he was considering whether to tell her that he never declared anything without a fault-free strategy already worked out. But he let that consideration slide away in favour of wondering what she would do if he leapt on her instead. She was already expecting it to happen, he could tell by the way she was sitting there tense, clutching her fingers together on her lap and with that invitingly curvy upper lip trembling in readiness of a full on sensual attack.

But it could wait—as *she* could wait until they were within reach of their bed. Though that did not mean he wasn't prepared to up the sensual ante a little. 'So you still only offer me the sex.'

'*Yes!*' Natasha insisted.

And only realised the trap she'd fallen into when he murmured softly, 'Good, because you look so beautiful tonight I ache to slide you out of that dress.'

His intentions declared, Leo left her to sizzle in her own strategic error as they arrived at his house. The heavy gates swung open. The car pulled to a stop at the bottom of the front steps. They both climbed out of it under their own steam, leaving Rasmus to slide the car out of their way so Natasha could cross the gap to Leo's side. He did not attempt to touch her as they walked up the steps and into the house. He let the stinging stitch of anticipation spin separate webs of expectation around both of them as they crossed the foyer and into the lift.

The moment they achieved the privacy of his floor Leo gave up on the waiting and reached for her—only Natasha took a swift step back.

'Tell me why you told everyone we are getting married,' she insisted.

His sigh was filled with irritation that she was persisting

with the subject. 'Because a formal announcement of our intention to marry will appear in all the relevant newspapers tomorrow, so I saw no reason to keep quiet about it,' he answered, and watched her delectable mouth drop.

'But you can't have done that without my say-so!'

'Well, I did.' He strode off, tugging impatiently at his bow tie.

Natasha hurried anxiously after him. 'But you can't have it both ways, Leo. You can't keep my relationship to Rico a secret to your friends *and* announce my name in the press at the same time!'

'You don't have a relationship with Rico.' The bow tie slid free of his shirt collar and was discarded onto a chair.

'Excuse me?' Natasha choked out. 'Aren't you the one who insists I'm Rico's thieving accomplice?'

He turned a steady look on her. 'Are you—his accomplice?'

Sheer angry cussedness made Natasha want to spit out a very satisfying *yes!* Then her innate honesty got the better of her. 'Not intentionally, no,' she answered wearily.

'Then do us both a favour and drop the subject.' As if he was bored with it, he shrugged out of his jacket. 'You were attacked tonight by a woman who cannot keep her husband in check and who is also a good friend of my ex-wife. I defended you. You should be feeling grateful, not screeching at me.'

It was the inference that she had been screeching that snapped Natasha's ready lips shut. Gianna was a screecher. Not in any way, shape or form did Natasha want to be compared with her!

It was only as she watched his hands move to the top button of his shirt that Natasha realised where they were standing in the bedroom and the need to keep fighting him withered right there.

She glanced at the bed, all neat and tidy with its corners turned down ready for them to slide between the cool white sheets. Her heart gave a flutter and she turned her gaze back onto Leo, who was calmly unbuttoning the rest of his shirt while he watched the telling expressions trip across her face.

'You led me in here deliberately,' she murmured.

His acknowledging smile was as lazily amused as hell. 'I am a natural tactician, *agape mou*. You should already know this.'

He was also the most sensuously beguiling man to watch undress. Natasha lost the thread of the conversation when her eyes fixed on the ribbon of hair-matted, bronzed flesh now on show down his front.

'You want to touch me?' The husky question in his voice made her lips tremble and part.

She couldn't even deny it with a shake of her head.

'Then come over here and touch me.' It was a soft-toned invitation—a darkly compelling masculine command.

And it tugged her towards him as if she were attached to him by invisible strings. She didn't even hate herself for giving in to it so easily, she just *wanted*—with a mind-blocking, sense-writhing need that brought her fingers up and reaching for him. He helped by taking hold of them and guiding them to his chest before he sank her into the warm, dark luxury of pleasure with the power of his kiss.

He peeled her out of her dress as promised. He stroked each satin curve of her body as if he were consigning each detail of her to memory, and eventually sank her down onto the bed.

'I shouldn't let you do this to me,' she groaned at one point when he made her feel as if she had molten liquid moving through her veins.

'You think I feel less than you do?' Catching one of her hands, he laid it against the pounding of his heart in his chest.

The rest of the night turned into long—long hours of slow loving. If Natasha had ever let herself wonder if there were really men out there that could sustain the flowing peaks of pleasure so often, then by the time they drifted into sleep she knew she need wonder no more.

Then the morning came, as bright and blue and glittering as the day before had been—only this morning Leo was tipping her unceremoniously out of the bed and pushing her into the bathrobe before dragging her out onto the terrace.

'What do you think you are doing?' Her sleep-hazed brain made her feel dizzy.

He made no answer, and there was no sign of the wonderfully warm and sensual man who'd loved her into oblivion the night before, just a cold, hard, angry male who pushed her down into a chair, then stabbed a finger at the newspaper he had folded open on the table in front of her.

'Read,' he said.

Read, Natasha repeated silently while still trying to get her muddy brain to work. He'd woken her up. He hadn't even let her use the bathroom. She could barely get her eyes to focus, never mind read a single thing!

Then she had no choice but to focus because the headline was typed in such bold black lettering it stabbed her with each soul-shattering, nerve-flaying word.

# CHAPTER EIGHT

LOVE CHEAT CHOOSES RICHES OVER RAGS! it yelled at her.

In an intriguing love triangle, Natasha Moyles—sister of Cindy Moyles, the new singing sensation everyone is talking about—has dumped the man she was supposed to be marrying in six weeks to run off with his Greek billionaire stepbrother, Leo Christakis, in a riches over rags love scandal that leaves the poorer Italian playboy Rico Giannetti out in the cold.

Cindy Moyles claims that she didn't see it coming. 'I had no idea that Natasha was seeing Leo Christakis behind Rico's back. I'm as shocked as everyone,' she insisted today as she sat with her new management team, who are about to launch her career with a new single predicted to clean up when it's released.

Rico Giannetti was not available for comment. His mother is said to be very upset. The Christakis PR department is denying there is anything untoward between their employer and his stepbrother's fiancée. However the picture below tells it all…

There was more—lots of it—but Natasha's eyes had stuck on the photograph showing her standing in a heated clinch with Leo right here on the balcony of this house. She was wrapped around him like a sex-hungry feline. There wasn't a hope that anyone was going to call it an innocent clinch.

'The beauty of power-zoom lenses,' Leo mocked from his lounging posture in the chair on the other side of the table.

With her face going white with shock to horror then heart-clutching dismay, she asked, 'But—how did they find out I was here with you?'

'Your sister,' he provided grimly. 'This is a very good example of damage limitation. Cindy's new management team is clearly on the ball. She must have gone straight to them with what happened and they got their heads together and decided to take the initiative by getting in her side of the story first. Fortunately for her I managed to gag Rico before she did or your dear sister placed herself at risk of coming out of this looking like the manipulative little whore that she is.'

'Don't say that.' Natasha felt stifled by the ugly picture he was painting. The truth was bad enough, but this made it all so much worse!

'Look at the evidence, Natasha,' he advised harshly. 'Look at the free publicity she is getting from this. Even her new management team has made sure their company name is printed.'

His angry tone made her shiver. 'Is there anything you can do to—?'

'Plenty of things,' he clipped in. 'I could strangle your sister, but I suspect it is already too late to do that. Or I could kick you out and allow myself the small satisfaction of knowing I will be painted as one hell of a ruthless bastard to have stolen you from beneath Rico's nose for the pleasure of a two-night stand! Being seen as that ruthless is good for my business image—the rest I don't give a toss about.'

Stung right through by his angry barrage, 'Or I could walk away under my own steam,' Natasha retaliated. 'I could play the true slut by making it known that I've had *both* brothers and neither were worth it!'

Across the table Leo's eyes darkened dangerously. Natasha didn't care. 'Well, think of it from my point of view,' she suggested stiffly. 'Miss Cool and Prim isn't quite as cool and prim as people like to think! I could make a small fortune selling my story—a juicy kiss-and-tell about the sexual antics of a billionaire tycoon and the poor Italian playboy!'

'Not worth it?' He picked up on the only part of what she'd thrown at him that seemingly mattered.

'I hate you,' she breathed, hunching inside her bathrobe. 'This was always going to get nasty. You carried me away on a cloud of assurances, but when I think back, you needed only half a minute once you'd got me into your house in London before you were flipping my head by telling me that you wanted me for yourself! What kind of man does that to a woman who'd just witnessed what I had witnessed? What kind of man picks her up and takes her to bed? What kind of man, Leo,' she thrust out furiously, 'propositions a woman, then carries through, knowing she was in no fit state to know what she was doing?'

'What kind of woman falls in love with a useless piece of pampered flesh like Rico and is too blind to notice he's still putting it out there with every female he can lay his hands on?'

Strike for strike, Leo cut deeper than anything she'd stabbed him with. Natasha tugged in a shuddering breath. 'I suppose next you're going to remind me that Rico didn't even want me.'

'So you can accuse me of accepting his unwanted cast offs?'

Natasha pushed to her feet on a daze of trammelled feelings. 'Is that how you see me?' she choked as last night's long loving strangled itself to death.

'No,' his voice rasped like coarse sandpaper across her ragged senses. 'I do not see you like that.'

'They why say it?' she shrilled out. 'Do you think I am

proud of the way I jumped into bed with you? Do you think I hadn't already worked out for myself that I was going to be labelled gold-digging tart for doing it?'

'Then why did you do it?'

He just didn't know when to leave something alone! Natasha's whole body quivered on the deep breath she took. 'Because you wanted me and I needed to be wanted.' And the devil himself couldn't tempt her to add that she'd been lost to reason from the moment their mouths had first touched. 'You get what you ask for,' she then mocked with weak tears thickening it. 'So, thank you, Leo, for taking such great care to teach me I am a normal sexual woman. I really do appreciate it.'

'My absolute pleasure,' he grimly silked out. 'But—to bring this discussion back to its original problem—there is one other option open to me that would save my face and your face.'

'W-what?' she couldn't resist prompting.

He laughed, low and deep and as sardonic as hell. 'A wedding,' he said as he picked up another newspaper, then leant forwards to place it on top of the other one. Instead of a tabloid, this one was a respected UK broadsheet, also conveniently folded at the right place.

It was the announcement of their forthcoming marriage. Natasha had forgotten all about it. Pressing her tense lips together, she made herself sit down and read it.

'It feels quite good to know that my instincts were working so well when I placed that in the papers,' Leo's dry voice delivered.

'I will still always look like a gold-digging tart with or without this.'

'Everyone loves a passionate romance, *agape mou*—so long as we do marry and make ourselves respectable, that is. It convinces the doubters that we cannot live without each other, you see. Of course,' he then added, 'you will have to agree to a gagging clause written into the prenuptial contract you are going to sign once my lawyers have drawn it up.'

And that, Natasha heard, was payback because she had just threatened to involve him in a kiss-and-tell exposé.

'Did you *know* about this tabloid article last night when we were dining with your friends?' she flashed out suddenly, though why the suspicion entered her head was beyond her capability to understand right now.

The velvet dark set of his eyes gave a surprised flicker before he carefully hooded them away. 'I happened to hear of it,' he disclosed coolly.

So he put out a counter-announcement declaring their intention to marry in a bid to make himself look better? Natasha threw herself back into her seat. 'You're as sly and manipulating as Cindy,' she quivered out in shaken dislike. 'God help us all if the two of you ever join up to make a team!'

'Your sister isn't my type. *You* are my type.'

The gullible type that didn't look around corners to see what others were hiding from her? Unable to stop the cold little shiver from tracking her spine, she said, 'A marriage between you and me is never going to work.'

Those sexy, heavy eyelids lifted upwards. 'Did I say I expected it to work?' he silked out.

As an image of the manic Gianna flashed across her eyes Natasha began to understand why the other woman—*wife*—of this man had turned so manic. He just didn't know when to quit with the knives!

'Marriage to Rico is starting to look more appetising by the minute,' she attacked back in muttering derision. 'At least he possessed *some* charm to offset the low-down, sneaky side to his character, whereas you—'

Leo was up out of his chair and looming over her before she could let out a startled shriek. 'You believe so?' he thinned out.

It was then that Natasha caught the glittering gold sparks burning up his eyes and remembered too late what it conveyed. The last time she'd seen that look she'd just accused him of being jealous of Rico, and his reaction then had—

'I was just kidding!' she cried out as his hands arrived around her waist and he hauled her bodily off the chair.

She found herself clamped to his front by a pair of arms that threatened to stop her breathing, her eyes on a level with his.

'I w-was just kidding, Leo,' she repeated unsteadily, forced to push her arms over his shoulders because there was nowhere else she could put them, and it didn't help that she was feeling the buzz, feeling the deep and pulsing, sense-vibrating buzz slink over each separate nerve-end as he held her gaze prisoner with the fierce heat of his next intention, turned with her and started walking them towards the curving glass.

And he didn't say a single word, which made the whole macho exercise even more exciting. He just tumbled her down onto the bed and followed her there, lips flat, face taut, his hands already making light of the belts holding their robes shut.

'Y-you deserved to hear it, though.' Natasha just could not resist adding fire to his anger. 'If—if you think about it, Leo, you're as ruthless ab-about getting what you want as—'

'Say his name again if you dare,' he breathed.

Natasha had the sense to block her tongue behind her teeth and knew she should be feeling alarmed and intimidated by his angry intent, but she didn't. She just lay there and let him part the two robes and waited for him to stretch out on top of her.

Heat by burning heat, their skin melded together at the same moment that his mouth took fierce possession of hers. And like someone who just did not know any better she fell into it all to kiss with every bit of aroused excitement at work inside her, hungry for him, greedy for him, slipping her legs around his waist so she could invite his full driving thrust.

He filled her and she loved it. He still held her eyes total prisoner as he moved in her with the deep and driven plunge of his hips. She loved that, too. Loved it so much she lifted her head to capture his mouth with short, soft, encouraging kisses that pulled a groan from his throat and sent his fingers spearing into her hair so he could hold her back to maintain the electrifying eye contact.

Nothing in her admittedly small experience warned her that the climax she was about to hit would turn her into a trembling state of shimmering static. Or that the man creating it was going to tremble in her arms.

When it was over, he lay heavy on her, his face buried in the heat-dampened hollow of her throat. Her heart was hammering, she could barely draw in her breath. What had just taken place had been so fevered and physical she lay there shell-shocked by the power of it. Every inch of her flesh still trembled, she could feel the same tremors still attacking him. And their limbs were tangled, the white towelling bathrobes generating a cocoon of intimacy all of their own.

When eventually he lifted his head to look down at her, the deep and intense darkness in his eyes snagged her breath all the more.

'I was rough with you,' he murmured unsteadily.

'No.' Natasha drew her hand up to rest it against his mouth. 'Don't say that,' she whispered. 'I—liked it.' And because she simply had to do it, she removed her hand and replaced it with the warm, soft tremor of her mouth.

One kiss led to another. Their robes disappeared. No matter how much angry passion had brought them back to this bed in the first place, this climb back through the senses was slow and deep and breathtakingly intense. He kissed her every-where and with complete disregard of any shyness she might have had left. She curled herself into him wherever she could do, she kissed and licked and bit his flesh and scored her hands over him, absorbing every pleasurable shudder he gave while whispering his name over and over again.

Afterwards was as if it weren't happening. They drifted with a silent sense of togetherness from the bed to the shower. In the husky deep voice of a man still in the power of what they'd created Leo showed her how to work the wet-room buttons and dials, then handed her a bar of soap and encouraged her to wash him while he stood, big shoulders pressed back against the white tiles with his eyes closed and his lean face stripped of its usual arrogance.

Natasha knew that something crucial had altered between them, though she could not put a name to what that something was.

Then—yes, she could, she thought as she leant in closer and moulded her lips around one of his tightly budded nipples. Somewhere during all of that intense loving, they had both dropped their guard.

Ages later, Leo dressed and went off to work and she—well, Natasha crawled back between the rumpled bedding, curled up on his side of the bed and whispered, 'I love him,' into his pillow.

It was shockingly, horribly that simple. She fell asleep wondering how she could have let it happen—and what the heck she was going to do about it....

That evening he took her out to dinner again. She chose to wear a little black dress that skimmed her curves rather than moulded them. As he ran his eyes over her, he lifted a hand up to absently stroke the bump in his nose and it struck

Natasha that he did that when he was unhappy about something—this time probably the little black dress.

Still, he chose to say nothing. He chose not to comment on the way she had pinned her hair up, leaving her neck and her shoulders bare. He wore a casual, taupe, linen suit and a black T-shirt that made her fingers want to stroke his front. He took her to a small, very select place in the hills outside the city away from the main tourist haunts. They ate food off a tiny candlelit table and drank perfectly chilled white wine. And each time she moved, the luxurious thickness of his eyelashes flowed down low over his eyes and she knew—just knew he was making love to her in his mind.

It was all so heady to be the total centre of his concentration like this. And the knowledge now that she was in love with him tugged and ached inside her so badly she was sure he must be able to tell in the husky quality of her voice and in her body language. Self-awareness became an irresistible drug that made her hold his attention with soft small talk and dark blue, tempting looks she didn't even realize she knew how to do.

Leo was captivated. She was so hooked on what was passing between them she was unaware how she'd drawn an invisible circle around the two of them. People he knew came up to speak to him. Natasha barely noticed. She barely heard the congratulations they were receiving or noticed the interested looks of speculation they sent her way. Whenever his attention was demanded elsewhere, he claimed her slender hand across the table and she even used this contact to keep his senses locked on her with the light brush of her fingers against his.

It was intoxicating to know that this beautiful and tantalising creature revealed herself only for him. To anyone else her responses were quiet and polite, but cool and reserved like the old Natasha. Rico had no idea what it was he had missed out on.

Rico. Leo flicked a hooded, dark glance at her and wondered how often his stepbrother's name crept into her head. Would she prefer to be sitting here with Rico? When she looked at him like this, was she secretly wishing that his face were Rico's face?

On a flick of tension he stood up suddenly and pulled her to her feet. 'Let's go,' he said.

He needed to be alone with her—in his bed.

'What's wrong?' Natasha asked him as Rasmus drove them down the hillside.

Leo didn't even turn his head to look at her, his long body sprawled in the seat beside her so taut she could almost feel the tension plucking at him.

'You are going to marry me whether you want to or not,' he announced coolly.

Silence clattered down around them, increasing the tension holding Leo, while he waited for her to shoot him down with a refusal as she usually did. When nothing came back at him he turned his head. She was sitting beside him with her spine a gentle curve into the leather seat and her eyes were fixed straight ahead. Everything about her was calm and still.

'Did you hear what I said?' he flicked out.

Lips forming the kind of lush, vulnerable profile that made him want to leap on them, she nodded her head.

'Then answer me,' he instructed impatiently.

'I was not aware that you had asked a question,' she responded dryly, 'more a statement of intent.'

'It will still require a *yes* from you when I drag you in front of a priest.'

So it will, Natasha thought with a wry kind of smile altering the contours of her mouth. Yesterday he'd made that shocking announcement to his friends and followed it up this morning with the printed version, tossed at her like a challenge, before coolly informing her that he did not expect a marriage between them to last. Then he'd taken her back to bed and seduced her into falling in love with him. He'd *made love* to her throughout the whole evening. Now the tough-talking man with a marriage ultimatum was back.

'Look at me, Natasha,' he commanded grimly.

She didn't want to look at him—but she still turned her head. It was like drowning in her own newly discovered feelings. Everything about him had become so overwhelmingly important to her in such a short space of time, she'd never felt so hopelessly helpless in her entire life.

'Marry me,' he repeated quietly.

'To help you save face?'

'No,' he denied. 'Because I want you to.'

It was like the final nail in the coffin of her resistance—not just the words he'd spoken, but the deep, dark, husky seriousness with which he had said them—and fed her with an oh-so-weak injection of hope.

'OK—yes,' she said.

OK—yes, he had to live with because, Leo acknowledged frustratingly, OK—yes, was all he was going to get. But he punished her for it later when they hit the bed.

He possessed her body and obsessed her senses, and Natasha let him. She had to because once she'd surrendered the marriage war she found she had no control left over with which to fight him about anything else.

And if this was real love, then it made her hurt like crazy, because, no matter how profoundly she knew she affected him, she also knew deep down inside her that the mind-blowing sex was as deep as it went for him.

Yet he rarely let her leave his side during the next couple of weeks leading up to their marriage. He took her with him wherever he went—even into his office sometimes, where she would stand by the window or sit in a chair and let him throw his weight around with the deeply resonant tone of his voice.

People got to know them as a couple so quickly, it came as no surprise that within days they were being talked about in Athens gossip press. Her betrothal to Rico came out for an airing and the 'riches over rags' label was just too good not to keeping using when they referred to her.

'Do you mind?' Leo asked her when one newspaper in particular did a real character assassination on her.

'It should be me asking you that question, since you don't come out of this any better than I do.'

'How can I mind? You did drop Rico, and you are here with me, and I am most definitely wealthier than Rico will ever be.'

And that was Leo, telling it as it was. Even Natasha couldn't argue with such simplicity and she knew the full truth.

There was no word from Rico. Natasha could find no photograph of him in any newspaper, and no one had tracked him down to get his comments on his broken engagement. He seemed to have dropped off the face of the earth.

Two weeks exactly from the day she had walked onto the Christakis private plane with Leo, Natasha married him in a quiet civil ceremony that took place in a closely guarded, secret location. She wore white—at his insistence—a strapless, French silk, tulle dress with a rouched bodice Persephone had found for her. When she stood beside Leo as they took their vows, he looked so much the tall, dark, sober-faced groom that she almost—almost lost courage and changed her mind.

The announcement of their marriage appeared in the next day's papers. By then they were already in New York. It was being called a honeymoon, but what it actually turned out to be was the beginning of a tour of Leo's business interests, which took them around the world. By day Leo played the powerful and cut-throat businessman, by night he played the suave sophisticate, socialising with business associates, and Natasha learnt to play the game at his side. While in the privacy of their bedroom, whichever country they were in, she played the lover to a man with an insatiably passionate desire for her.

From New York to Hong Kong to Tokyo then Sydney. By the time they landed back on Greek soil two more weeks had gone by and Natasha was such a different person she could barely remember the one she used to be.

But, more than that, she had allowed herself to forget the real reasons why they had embarked on this marriage in the first place.

She received her first jolting reminder as they walked through the airport and passed an English newspaper stand. She saw Cindy's name and face splashed across every magazine, celebrating her first UK number-one hit.

'So she got her dearest wish,' Leo remarked dryly.

'Yes,' Natasha answered, staring at the way Cindy looked so different, more like a beautiful and youthful, blue-eyed blonde with no hint of her old angst or petulance in sight.

Cindy had pulled on a new persona just as she had, Natasha likened. Whether it went further than skin-deep with her sister was a question she was not likely to find the answer to because Cindy belonged in her past now.

The next stark reminder as to what she'd left behind in England came amongst the stack of congratulation cards they found waiting for them at the house. This particular one stood out from the rest because she recognised the writing and it was addressed only to her. Inside was a traditionally standard greeting card with silver embossed wedding bells on the front and a simple message of congratulations printed inside. It was from her parents, with a brief note written in her mother's hand.

'We wish you every happiness in your marriage,' was all that it said. No loving endearments, no sign that she had ever been their daughter at all.

'Perhaps they know they treated you badly and don't know how to say so,' Leo suggested quietly.

'And perhaps they're just relieved to bring closure to a twenty-four-year-old mistake.' Turning the envelope over, she frowned at it. 'I wonder how they managed to get hold of this address?'

'Angelina,' Leo provided the answer. 'They have been—keeping in touch.'

That brought Natasha's attention up to his face. 'And you knew this but didn't think to tell me?'

'What was there to tell?' he answered with a shrug. 'Angelina needed to ensure her son was not pilloried in the press by an enterprising Cindy. Your parents needed to ensure that Cindy was not pilloried by a bitter Rico out to get his revenge.'

'You mean, Cindy *did* set him up?'

'Whoever made the first move, *agape mou*, it happened.'

And that was Leo at his tell-it-as-it-is best.

Natasha slipped the card back in its envelope and did not look at it again.

Another week went by and Leo was busy with a major takeover he'd been working on while they'd travelled the world. Now they were back in Athens, he was devoting his whole time to it, busy, preoccupied, some nights not coming home at all because he had to fly off to one place or another to meet with people, which meant an overnight stay.

The fact that he didn't take her with him on these occasions didn't worry Natasha at all. She had other things to think about. She might have let Leo pay for all the expensive de-signer stuff she now wore with such ease and indifference, but she paid for everything else herself. Now her small nest of savings had shrunk so small she needed to find a job.

Anything would do, she wasn't picky. She soon discovered, though, that without even a smattering of Greek in her vocabulary she was pretty much unemployable in a formal office environment. So she started trawling the tourist spots hoping someone would like to employ an Englishwoman with reasonable intelligence and a pleasant speaking voice.

Leo found out about what she was doing. They had their first major row in weeks. He had the overbearing nerve to prohibit *his wife* from working in such menial employment as a tourist shop. He would increase her allowance if she was so strapped for cash, he said.

'Don't you think I *know* I owe you enough money already without letting you shell out even more?'

Saying it out loud like that hit both of them harder than either of them expected. In one week she would have been marrying Rico. In one short week she could access the money locked up in the offshore account.

Leo just stared at her coldly, then spun on his heel and walked away. Natasha felt as if she'd just murdered something special, but the truth was the truth and she had to face up to that.

By telling it as it is, she thought heavily. She'd been taught by a master at it, after all.

The long, swooping dive down into reality began from that moment on. For the next few days they lived in a state of unarmed combat, in which Leo made himself scarce—being busy—and Natasha job-hunted with a grim determination not to let him dictate to her, by working her way along the tourist shops in the Plaka through the stifling heat of a melting July, perfectly aware of the minder Leo had put on her to track her every move.

It had to be the worst luck in the world when she literally bumped right into his ex-wife, Gianna, as she was coming out of one shop, still unemployed, hot, tired and miserable with it. Maybe the meeting had been contrived. How was she to know? But the way Gianna stopped her from walking right past her by clipping her long fingernails to Natasha's arm was enough to make her wonder if the dark beauty had been waiting to pounce.

'I want to talk to you,' Gianna said thinly.

'I don't think so.' Natasha tried to move on, but the nails dug in deeper to keep her still.

'Leo is mine!' Gianna spat at her. 'You think you have him caught with that ring on your finger, but you do not. You think with your cool blonde looks you are the perfect antidote to me, but Leo has always and will always belong to me!'

'Not so anyone would notice,' Natasha responded, refusing to be shaken by the venom in Gianna's voice. 'As you say, I wear his ring now. *I* sleep in his bed. And I *don't* pass myself around his friends!'

Even Natasha could not believe she'd said that. Gianna responded with a laugh that went with the wildly hysterical look in her eyes. She unclipped her fingernails and for a second Natasha thought she was going to score them down her face. She even took a jerky step back, sensed her minder step in closer to her and watched Gianna's top lip curl in scorn.

'You little fool,' she said. 'Where do you think he spends his nights when he is not with you?'

'That's a lie,' Natasha breathed, not even giving the suggestion room to apply its poison and sending Gianna a pitying look. 'Get some help, Gianna,' she advised coldly. 'You desperately need it.'

Then she beat a hasty retreat, with her minder tracking in her shadow as she disappeared into the crowds, angrily refusing to rub her arm where the other woman's fingernails had bit.

Leo was waiting for her when she got back to the house. Grim as anything, he didn't say a single word, but just took possession of her arm and turned it to inspect the angry red crescents embedded in her smooth white skin.

'How did you find out?' Natasha asked as she watched his fingertips lightly stroke the red marks.

'Does it matter?'

'No.' Natasha sighed, remembering the minder by then anyway. 'I think she's stark staring mad and I actually feel very sorry for her.'

'Well, don't,' he said. 'Believe me, it is dangerous to feel sorry for Gianna.'

'Thanks for the warning.' She took her arm back. 'Now you've checked I'm not bleeding to death, you can go back to work.'

It was the way she said it that rang a familiar bell inside Leo's head. He took a step back to look at her. She was *not* looking at him. And if he had been wondering lately if the old Natasha had gone for ever, with that cool remark he discovered that she had not.

He heaved out a sigh. He'd had a lousy week. Several times the takeover had threatened to go stale and he'd had to fly off somewhere at the last minute to affect a recovery. Normally he thrived on the cut-and-thrust challenge of testing deals like this. It was what made his hunter's instincts tick. But it was only now as he stood here listening to Natasha's cool attempt to dismiss him that he realised how much he had missed using his hunter's instinct on her.

'You want to indulge in another argument?' he prompted smoothly.

'No.' She turned her back as if meaning to walk away from him.

'You want to come to bed with me, then, and spend the afternoon showing me how much you wish I did not have to fly to Paris tonight?'

'Paris?' That swung her back to face him. 'But you've only just got back from there yesterday!'

'And now I must go back there tonight.' His elegant shrug made light of the constant travelling his job demanded, but the look in his eyes did not make light of what was now going on in his head.

Natasha folded her arms across her front. 'Is that why you're here—to pack a bag?'

Playing the provoking innocent just flew right over Leo's head because he could read her body language and those folded arms were no protection at all from what he was generating here. 'I was thinking more on the lines of—something different,' he silked out, closing the gap between them like a big, dark and hungry, stalking cat. 'I have this bottle of champagne on ice, you see, no glasses and several novel ways of enjoying it, if you are interested, that is…'

Natasha couldn't help it, she laughed. 'You're shocking—'

'You love me to be shocking.' He took hold of her wrists and gently unlinked her arms. 'It's what makes you give in so easily when I do this…'

And she did give in. She let him possess her mouth and take her to bed and she let him spend the afternoon shocking her, because she wanted him and she'd missed making love with him and…

The power of a poisoned barb, she heard herself think heavily at one point within the sensual haze he'd wrapped her in and knowing that there was a small part of her that let him do this to her because Gianna's comments made her want to send him away to Paris so totally satiated he wouldn't need to look elsewhere for this.

They stayed hidden in the bedroom throughout the afternoon and she could tell that he did not want to go when it was time for him to leave.

'Will you do me a big favour, and take a day off from job-hunting tomorrow?' he requested.

Her stubborn pout was the beginning of a refusal, which he kissed away.

'Please?' he added when he lifted his head again.

'One good reason,' she bargained, slender white fingertips toying with his smoothly shaved face.

Did he remind her that tomorrow was the day she would have been marrying Rico? Leo brooded. And knew it wasn't really a question because the last thing he wanted to do was to leave her here in his bed thinking about his stepbrother instead of him.

'Because I will be back by lunch with a surprise for you...' catching hold of her caressing fingers, he kissed them '...but only if you are right here waiting for me when I get back.'

'Ah,' said Natasha. 'Blackmail is much more your style. It had better be a good surprise, then.'

Leo just smiled as he rose to his impressive six feet four inches of pure arrogant male in a suit. His gaze lingered, though, on the way she was lying there like a fully-fledged siren stretched out on his bed with her tumbled hair and provoking blue eyes and sumptuously kissed, reddened mouth.

'Where did I get the impression that you were a prude?' he mocked as his gaze slid lower over the creamy fullness of her breasts with their tempting pink centres, and the cluster of dusky blonde curls delineating the heart-shaped juncture with her slender white thighs.

Impulse made him lean down again and place a kiss on that cluster, his tongue darting down in a claim of possession that caused one of those delicious quivers of pleasure she was so free with him.

'See you tomorrow,' he murmured, and left the room before he changed his mind about going anywhere, taking with him the confidence that his woman would be thinking only of him until they came together again.

Natasha slept fitfully that night because she missed him beside her. And awoke the next morning with a thick headache that made her decide to take the day off from job hunting as Leo wanted her to do, which should please him—she thought with a smile.

She was lingering over a solitary breakfast when her mobile phone started to ring. So sure it was going to be Leo calling her, she snatched it up and answered it without checking who it was.

So it came as a shock when it was Cindy's voice that jarred her eardrum.

# CHAPTER NINE

'What do you want?' Natasha demanded coldly.

She heard her sister's sigh of relief. 'I wasn't sure you still used this mobile number,' Cindy explained the relieved sigh.

Natasha said nothing, just lowered her eyes to watch the way her fingers stroked the frosted dampness from her glass of orange juice and let the silence stretch.

'OK, so you don't want to speak to me,' Cindy acknowledged. 'But I need to talk to you, Natasha, ab about the parents.'

Natasha's fingers went still. 'Why—what's wrong with them?'

'Nothing—*everything*,' Cindy sighed out. 'Look…I'm in Athens. I flew in this morning without telling anyone I was coming here, and I have to be back in London this afternoon before I'm missed. Will you meet with me to—talk about them? Trust me, Tasha, it's important or I would not be here.'

Which told her that Cindy wanted this contact no more than she did. But if she'd flown all the way just to speak to her, then whatever she needed to say had to be serious.

Her parents—her parents…that weakness called love gave an aching squeeze. 'OK,' she agreed. 'Do you want to come here so we can—'

'Good grief, no,' Cindy shuddered out. 'I have no desire

to bump into Leo, thank you very much. He gives me the heebie-jeebies.'

'He isn't here.'

'I still won't take the risk. I hired a limo at the airport. Just name a location away from your place and I will get my driver to take me there.'

Natasha glanced at her watch, then named a café in Koloniki Square, and heard Cindy consulting with her driver before she said, 'OK. We can be there in an hour.'

It did not occur to Natasha to question the *we* part. It did not occur to her to question why her totally selfish-seeking sister would come all the way here from England to discuss their parents when it would have been so much quicker and easier for her to just say it on the phone. It was only when she sat waiting at a café table beneath the shade of a leafy tree and watched a silver limo pull up at the edge of the square, then a man climb out of it instead of her sister, that she realised just how thoroughly she had allowed herself to be duped.

Natasha stood up, her first instinct being to just walk away! Then curiosity made her go still as she watched Rico pause to look around him, his eyes hidden behind a pair of silver-framed sunglasses as he scanned the whole square until he located Natasha's minder, then took a quick glance at his watch before he continued towards her.

Dressed in a designer casual pale linen suit and a plane white T-shirt, he looked his usual fashion-plate self. His black hair shone like silk in the sunlight and there wasn't a female in the vicinity from the age of nine to ninety that didn't turn and stare.

But then that was Rico, Natasha thought as she watched him. She, too, had fallen instant victim to his amazing good looks and that special aura he carried everywhere with him, so it was no use her pretending it wasn't there. Except—as she looked at him now she felt absolutely nothing. It was like looking at a stranger—a great-looking stranger, she still had to allow, but a total stranger nonetheless.

When he reached her table, Natasha sat back down in her chair and waited for him to take the seat.

'Still hating me, *cara*?' he drawled as his opening volley.

'Isn't Cindy going to join us?' was all she said in return.

'No.' Leaning back in the chair, Rico glanced at Natasha's minder, who was already talking into his mobile phone.

'I would say you have about five minutes to say what you've set me up to say,' Natasha offered up helpfully.

Looking back at her, Rico pulled off his sunglasses and something strange appeared in the dark brown depths of his eyes. 'You look different,' he murmured. 'That dress suits you.'

'Thank you.' Natasha was not in the least bit impressed by the compliment since the dress was a simple coffee-coloured shift thing she had chosen at random and with no intent to impress anyone.

'I think I should...'

'Get straight to the point,' she suggested. 'Since neither of us want to watch Leo appear in his three-car cavalcade.'

Rico grimaced, clearly understanding exactly what it was she was referring to. One of his hands went into his inside jacket pocket and came out with a folded set of documents.

'All I need you to do, Natasha, is put your signature on these, then I will be out of here.'

He laid a set of papers down on the table in front of her, then followed them with a pen. Natasha looked down, understanding instantly what it was he was expecting her to sign.

She looked back at him. 'Would you like to explain to me why you think I should sign these?'

He shifted his wide shoulders. 'Because the money does not belong to you,' he replied with the absolute truth. 'I want it now that it's accessible.'

He didn't know that she knew where the money had come from, Natasha realised. Leo could not have told him, which left her wondering why he hadn't, and what she was supposed to do next.

Her eyes flickered over to where the silver limo was still parked with its tinted windows denying her a glimpse inside. 'Did you convince Cindy to get you this meeting by threatening to give the true story about her involvement with you to the press?'

Rico offered another shrug. 'I lost everything while she gained everything. You tell me if that was fair? Your sister got her record contract and her number-one hit. I got to be laughed at for losing my woman to my big-shot stepbrother.'

'I was never yours in the true sense, Rico,' Natasha reminded him.

He ignored that. 'Leo put me out of a job with no damn reference and I am suddenly persona non grata in every social circle that counts. Even my own mother doesn't like me right now and you sit here looking like a million dollars because Leo likes his women to look worthy of him. But I hope you are happy with him, *cara*, while you share him with his sex-mad ex-wife.'

With a flip of a long, graceful hand, Rico dropped his flashy, state-of-the-art phone down on the table in front of her. 'Take a look,' he invited.

Natasha's eyelashes quivered as she dropped her gaze to the phone. She didn't want to pick it up. She didn't want to look. A cold chill was beginning to freeze her heart muscles because she knew Rico wasn't inviting her to check out his phone for fun, just as he hadn't mentioned Gianna without a reason for doing it.

Even her fingers felt chilled by the time they made a trembling crawl towards the phone and hit the key that would light the screen up. Leo appeared in stark digital clarity with the beautiful Gianna plastered to his front. They were standing outside what looked like a hotel. 'Leo, please,' she heard Gianna's pleading voice arrive in her ears in a near-perfect English speaking voice. 'She does not have to know!'

In full gut-churning colour, she watched Leo smile, watched him run a finger along the lush red contours of Gianna's beautiful mouth. 'OK.' He leant down to kiss that pleading mouth. 'I will come in with you.'

Then they walked up the steps and into the hotel.

'Paris,' Rico answered the question Natasha was trying so hard not to let herself think. 'Last night, to be exact. You can check the date and time if you like,' he indicated to the phone. 'I hung around for two hours waiting for him to come out again, but he didn't. You tell me, *cara*, what you think they were doing with those two hours?'

Natasha didn't answer. She was recalling another scene weeks ago, when she had stood in Rico's office doorway watching *his* betrayal of her drag the blind scales from her eyes. In this case it was Rico's telephone that formed the doorway from which she watched this new betrayal.

Without saying a word she put down the mobile and picked up Rico's pen.

Natasha just scrawled her name on the document, then she got up and walked away.

If she'd looked back she would have seen her minder pausing beside Rico's chair—but she didn't look back. She didn't even offer a sideways glance at the silver limo as she walked past it.

Leo arrived home as she was packing her bag. He came in through the bedroom door like a bullet, a seething mass of barely controlled fury trapped inside a sleek dark business suit.

'What the hell were you doing with Rico?' he bit out.

Natasha didn't answer; she just turned back to her bag.

'I asked you a question!' He arrived at her side and caught hold of her arm to swing her around. It was only as he did so that his eyes dropped to the bag she was packing. Cold fury suddenly lit him up. 'If you think you are leaving me for him you can think it through again,' he raked out.

Natasha just smiled.

The smile hit him as good as a hard slap. 'You bitch,' he choked, tossing her arm aside and reeling away from her. 'I can't believe you could do this to me.'

'Why not?' Natasha let herself speak at last—and the hell if she was going to tell him what she knew about him and Gianna. Let him know what it feels like to have his pride shredded!

It was like watching a mighty rock turn into an earthquake. The shudder that shook him almost shook her, too. 'You signed the money over to him,' he stated hoarsely.

'Yes, I did, didn't I?' she said smoothly. 'Are you going to inform the police?'

His bunched shoulders tensed. 'You're my wife.'

'So I am.'

He swung back, his angry eyes sharpened by the dry tone in her voice. 'What the *hell* is that supposed to imply?'

Natasha offered a shrug. 'Our marriage was just a form of blackmail you used to bring darling Gianna into line, so I don't think it counts as anything much.'

'Don't change the subject. Gianna has nothing to do with this.'

'She has everything to do with it!' Natasha cried out, then took a deep breath and pulled herself together again because she was close to telling him what she knew and she didn't want to do that. She *never* wanted him to know how much he had hurt her today! 'I was there, if you recall. Until she turned up, I was just the little thief you took to your bed to enjoy for six weeks until you got your precious money back. The marriage thing came up as one of your smart-mouthed quips aimed to punish your silly ex-wife for barging in while you were busy with me!'

'That's not true.'

'It is true,' she insisted. 'What was it you said to me before we left London, Leo? Six weeks keeping you sweet in your bed until I could access your money, then I was gone? Well, the six weeks are up. I've accessed the money and now I'm leaving.'

With that she turned back to pick up her holdall. He was at her side before she had touched the strap. The packed bag went flying to the floor. Natasha barely managed a quivering gasp of protest before he was spinning her round to face him again. Black fury was firing from his every skin cell. She had never seen his eyes so hard. He was white—ghost white. He was even shaking as he held her.

'To go back to him?' he shot out.

Eyes like iced-blue glass, she gave him his answer. 'Well, you of all people must know what they say about the devil you know,' she provoked.

She was referring to Gianna and he knew that she was. His eyes gave a blinding bitter flash of instant understanding. 'You know about Paris.'

He was that quick-thinking, the rotten, cruel, heartless swine! 'I hate you, Leo,' she shook out thickly. 'You're a cold and hard, calculating devil. For all his faults, Rico is worth ten of you!'

'You think so?'

'I know so!' Natasha tried to pull free of him.

His fingers tightened. 'Say hello to this devil, then,' he gritted, then his mouth landed on hers like a crushing blow.

They'd kissed in anger before and turned the whole thing into a glorious fight, but this was different. Natasha didn't want this, but her body was not listening. She hated him with every spinning atom of her being but one touch from him lit her up like a torch. And her thin dress was no barrier to help shield her. He dealt with it by the simple method of wrenching the back zip apart so the dress fell in a slither to the ground.

'Get off me!' she choked at him.

'When you stop wanting me so desperately,' he rasped back.

Then he was kissing and touching and caressing and *goading* her to reject what he knew she could not! He knew every weak inch of her. He stripped away her clothes and aroused her with a grim ruthlessness that had her whimpering against his possessing mouth. And when that wasn't enough for him, he lifted her up against him, making her straddle his hips while his mouth maintained the deep, driving possession of her mouth.

Next thing she knew she was being dropped on the bed while he stood over her, holding her still by the sheer power of his angry desire-blackened gaze as he stripped off his clothes. The jacket, the shirt—shoes heeled off and flicked out of his way. When he stripped the last garments away, he was like a menacing threat that completely dominated her every thought and sense, and tingling tight fear cloaked her in sizzling excitement.

'Leo—please…' she begged in an appeal for sanity.

'Leo—please…' he mimicked tautly. 'You have no idea what it does to me when you say that.'

Then he came over her, arriving on the bed. With a bewilderingly slick show of controlled strength Natasha found her thighs smoothly parted and he was lowering his angry dark head. 'Make sure you tell Rico all about this later,' he muttered.

What took place next cast her into an agony of skin-tingling pleasure. She moved and groaned and sobbed and shuddered and he just went on doing it, keeping her finely balanced on the edge of frantic hysterics and a clamouring, desperate need for release. If she tried to protest he snaked up and kissed her. If she tried to get away, he stayed her with the clamp of his hands to her hips. When he finally decided it was time to join them, his first driving thrust made her cry out in soul-crushing relief. Then he was lifting her up and tipping her head back so he could devour her mouth while he rode her like that, with her hair flowing behind her and her fingers clinging to the sinew-tight tension in his neck. The angry glare in his eyes would have been frightening if it weren't for the glaze of hot, urgent desire that matched the quick, deep, thrusting drive of his hips as he brought them both rushing towards the pinnacle of a nerve-screeching release.

When it came, she arched like a slender bow strung so tight she couldn't relax again. The stinging whip-crack of her orgasm played through her in a series of violent, electric shocks as Leo let go with a single powerful quake of his body. The whole wild seduction with its total breakdown of control had taken just a few short dizzying minutes, yet when it was over, Natasha felt as if she'd been scraped clean of energy, exhausted of the strength to even move.

Not so Leo. On a thick growl of contempt he withdrew from her and climbed off the bed. Whether the contempt had been aimed at her or at himself didn't matter. The way he picked up his clothes and left her lying there in a weak, quivering huddle and just strode out of the room riddled her with contempt for herself.

Natasha continued to lie there for ages, trying to come to terms with what had happened—trying to come to terms with the whole barbaric crescendo ending to their relationship. She hated herself for falling victim too easily. She despised him for encouraging it. When she could find the strength to move, she just got off the bed, got dressed in the first clothes that came to hand, then repacked her bag with only the clothes she'd brought with her to Greece.

Then she left. Nobody tried to stop her from going. She didn't even bother to ring for a taxi before she stepped outside and walked down the drive towards the pair of gates. The guard on the gate said absolutely nothing, but just opened them and let her into the street.

Leo stood in front of the curving glass wall and watched her do it. She hadn't even stopped long enough to tidy her hair, he saw, and she was wearing that damn pale blue suit.

He turned away from the window, bitterness warring with an agony that was tightening the muscles lining his throat. He looked at the tangle of sheets on the bed.

Then he saw the manila envelope lying there on top of the bedding. As he walked over to it and saw *'Leo'* scrawled on it he felt his legs turn hollow with dread as he picked the envelope up.

A cruising taxi picked Natasha up and a few minutes later she was heading for the airport without allowing herself a single glance back. It was only when she sat back in the seat that she noticed she was wearing the pale blue suit.

Fitting, she thought bleakly. Maybe the suit should be preserved in a glass case to remind her that she was a fool and all men were lying cheats.

The airport was busy. Trying to get a seat on a flight back to England was impossible, she discovered, beginning to wilt now as that first rush of adrenalin that had carried her this far began to ebb.

'You can only hope for a cancellation, Kyria Christakis,' the booking agent told her. 'Otherwise we have no seat available for the next two days.'

'W-what about a different airport?' Her voice was beginning to shake, Natasha noticed. She could feel a bubble of hysteria fighting to burst free from her throat. 'M-Manchester, perhaps, or Glasgow. I don't really care where I land so long as it is on UK soil.'

What was there in London for her to go back to anyway? she was just asking herself when a hand arrived on her shoulder.

Natasha jumped like a scalded cat as her mind threw up a terrifying image of the hand belonging to the police.

He wouldn't—he *wouldn't*! her mind screamed at her.

Then the voice came. 'That will not be necessary.'

# CHAPTER TEN

As NATASHA trembled in recognition, Leo's hand became an arm clamping around her shoulders that contained her tense tremor within the power of his grasp. She was engulfed within seconds, by his height, by his strength, by his grim determination and by the cool use of his native language as he spoke to the curious booking agent while Rasmus appeared beside her and calmly bent to claim her bag.

'No...' She tried to stop him. 'I don't w-want—'

'Don't make a fuss, *agape mou*,' Leo murmured levelly. 'We are under surveillance from the Press.'

She was suddenly surrounded by his security men. Before she'd grasped what was happening they were hustling her through the airport like a human bulldozer, which gave her no view as to where they were going, and the tight grip Leo maintained on her kept her clamped against his side.

Gates magically opened for them. Having thought he was taking her back to his apartment, it came as a hard shock to find herself walking across tarmac towards what looked like a helicopter from the brief glimpse she caught of the rotor-blades already beginning to turn as they approached.

Panic erupted. 'I am not getting on that with you!' She pulled to a shuddering halt, causing men to struggle not to bump into her.

Breaking free of his grip, she spun back the way they had come. Leo bit out a command that sent burly men scattering. He hauled her up off her feet and into his arms, then completed the rest of the distance between them and the helicopter with the grim surefootedness of a man happy to dice with death by rotor-blade.

Natasha ducked her head into his shoulder in sheer fright and did not lift it up again until he'd put her down on a seat. The moment he let go of her she hit out at him with her fists.

He chose not to notice as he grimly fastened her into the seat while her angry blows just glanced off him. 'I hate you, *I hate you*!' she kept choking out.

'Save it until later,' he responded, and she'd never seen his face look so tough.

'But why are you doing this?'

He didn't answer, just stepped back to allow six men to pile in the helicopter, swarming like black-suited rats into the seats in front of her and behind. Natasha felt so wretchedly deserted and so terrified that Leo was going to send her off somewhere with his men so that they could deal with her, she couldn't stop herself from crying out, 'Leo—*please* don't leave me with them!'

By then he had his back to her. His wide shoulders gave a tense flex, but he did not turn around. Without offering her a single word of reassurance he just strode round the helicopter and climbed in the seat beside the pilot. In what felt like no time at all they were up in the air and shooting forwards towards the glinting blue of the Aegean. Natasha closed her eyes and tried hard not to let the panic inside her develop any more than it had done already. At least he was in here with her, she told herself fiercely. Whatever else that was happening, *at least* he wasn't leaving her to the care of his horrible men!

Leo dared a brief glance at her via the mirror positioned above the cockpit controls. Her eyes were shut tight, her lips parted and trembling and pale, and she had gone back to clutching her damn purse to her lap as if it were her only lifeline. The blue suit, the purse, the expression—all of them reminded him of the last time he'd virtually abducted her like this.

Except for the hair. The hair was free and tumbling around her stark white beautiful—*beautiful* face!

Hell, damn it. *Theos* help me! he thought angrily as his insides creased up, and he had to look away from her.

His pilot said something. He didn't hear what it was. He was so locked into one purpose it left no room in his head for anything else.

It did not take long to reach their destination. They touched down as the sun was turning everything a warm golden red. Even as they settled onto the ground he could see Natasha struggling to unlock her seat belt and—*hell*, maybe he should just let her escape because he knew he was in no fit state of mind to be safe around her right now.

Rasmus undid the seat belt for her because she couldn't seem to do it. It was from within a dazed state that Natasha stared at her fingers, which seemed to have turned to trembling jelly with no hope of control left. All of her felt that way, when she thought about it.

Rasmus also helped her down onto solid ground with an unusual gentleness for such a tough man. When she glanced up at him to whisper a shaky, 'Thank you,' he sent her the strangest apologetic look.

For some reason that look almost finished her. The tears were suddenly flooding upwards in a hot, raging gush. She turned away from him, not wanting Rasmus to see the tears—not wanting to see his apology! Leo appeared around the nose of the helicopter looking exactly like the tall, dark, tough stranger she used to see him as.

He needed a shave, she noticed hazily. And he was wearing the same clothes he had picked up off the bedroom floor. They looked creased and dishevelled. *He* looked creased and dishevelled.

Her stomach dipped and squirmed but she refused to analyse why.

And she dragged her eyes away from Leo, too.

He didn't touch her.

'Shall we go?' he said, and took an oddly formal step to one side in a silent invitation for her to precede him.

Where to, though? Natasha wondered anxiously as her reluctant feet moved her ahead of him, hating him like poison for doing this to her, and despising him further for bringing her down to the point that she had cried out to him in fear.

They rounded a tall hedge and suddenly she was faced with a rambling two-storey villa with sun-blushed white walls. No housekeeper waited to greet them. Everyone else seemed to have just melted away. Leo stepped in front of her to open the front door, then he led the way across a soft eggshell blue and cream hallway and into the kind of living room you only usually saw in glossy magazines.

'Wh-what is this place?' Natasha could not stop herself from asking, looking round her new surroundings that were as different again from the two other places Leo taken her to. Not a hint of the old-fashioned heaviness of the London house here, and it was certainly no ultra-modern, urban dwelling aimed to please the eye of the wealthy male.

No, this place was pure classical luxury with stunning artwork hanging on the walls and pieces of handmade furniture that must have cost the earth.

'My island retreat,' Leo answered, removing the jacket to his suit and slinging it over the back of a chair.

His *island* retreat, as in his *whole* island retreat?

In other circumstances Natasha would have been willing to be impressed by that, but she refused to be impressed by anything he said or did from now on—other than to give some answers to the real questions running round in her head.

Standing still just inside the doorway, she clutched her purse in her fingers and lifted up her chin. 'So is this to be my new luxury prison?' she iced out.

'No.' He moved across the room to pour himself a drink.

'You mean, I get to leave it whenever I want to, then?'

She saw his grim mouth flex at her sarcasm. 'No,' he said again.

'Then it's a prison.' She looked away from him.

To her absolute shock, he slammed the glass down and turned to stride back across the room to pull her into his arms and kiss her—hard.

There had never been a kiss like it. This one seemed to rise up from some deep place inside him and flow with a throbbing heat of pure feeling aimed to pour directly into her. It shook Natasha, really shook her. When he put her from him, she could only stare up at him in a bewildered daze.

He turned his back on her. 'Sorry,' he muttered. 'It was not my intention to—'

Like a woman living in some kind a surreal alternative life, Natasha could only stumble into the nearest chair.

'I don't understand what's going on here,' she whispered when he just stood there like a stone pillar. 'You kidnap me from the airport and hustle me like a piece of cattle onto your helicopter and scare me out of my w-wits. Then you bring me in here and *dare* to kiss me like that!'

He didn't speak. He didn't turn. His hands clenched into

fists, then disappeared into his trouser pockets. She noticed that his shirt cuffs were hanging open around his wrists.

'What else do you want from me, Leo?' she cried out in a thick voice.

'Nothing,' he said, his big shoulders flexing. 'I don't want anything else from you. I just don't want you to leave me.'

Then he really bewildered her by striding towards a pair of French windows and throwing them open so he could go outside.

Natasha stared after him and wished she understood him. Then on a sudden rush of angry hot blood she decided that she didn't *want* to understand a man like Leo, she just wanted him to explain that last remark!

Getting up on legs that did not want to carry her anywhere, she followed him outside and found herself stepping onto a deep terrace. The sun was hanging so low in the sky now it blinded her eyes. But she could see enough to know that Leo wasn't here. Casting her gaze out wider, she caught sight of his white shirt moving down through a garden towards the ocean gleaming a deep silken blue not far away.

By the time she reached a low wall that kept the beach back from the gardens, he was standing at the water's edge, hands still pushed into his pockets, staring out to sea.

'What is it with you?' she demanded. 'Why are you doing this to me? If it's because of the money, you only—'

'I don't want the money.'

Natasha paused several feet away from him. 'You found the envelope, then?' He just nodded. She let out a sigh. 'Then what do you want?' she asked helplessly.

Still he made no answer and the tears started coming again. Any second now he was going to succeed in completely breaking her control. Maybe that was what he wanted, she thought as she sank down on the low wall because her legs had finally given in.

'You're so arrogant, Leo,' she said unsteadily. 'You're so cynical about everyone and everything. You see no good in anyone. You believe everyone out there is trying to fleece you in one way or another. Y-your ex-wife wants your body, I want your money, Rico wants to stand in your shoes and *be* you. If you want my opinion, you would be better off poor and downright ugly—then at least you could be happy knowing no one liked you for just being you!'

He laughed when he wasn't meant to. Natasha had to swallow on the lump her throbbing heart had become in her throat. 'You just love it when you think s-someone has proved your every cynical suspicion about them true.'

'Are you referring to what happened this afternoon?'

So he speaks! Natasha glared at him but couldn't see him through the bank of tears misting up her eyes. 'Yes,' she said, though that wasn't all of it. 'You came into our bedroom today expecting to see a cheating wife so you treated m-me like a cheating wife.'

'I thought you had signed the money over to Rico. It—hurt me.'

'Not enough to make you demand a proper explanation before you drew your own conclusions, though.'

Then she tensed warily as he spun on his heel, crunching gravelly sand beneath his shoes as he did.

'What did you sign for Rico?' he asked curiously.

'Permission to access an empty offshore account,' she answered with a shrug. 'I'd already transferred the money over to my private bank account yesterday. I meant to give you the envelope with the banker's draft in it yesterday but we were—sidetracked.'

By Gianna first, she remembered bleakly, then by an afternoon of—

Something dropped onto her lap and made her blink. 'W-what's this?' Warily she picked up the narrow white envelope.

'Take a look.'

Natasha looked at the envelope for what felt like ages before she could get her fingers to slip the seal. Her lips felt so dry she had to moisten them with her tongue as she removed the contents. It was getting really dark out here now, but still light enough for her to recognise what it was she was looking at.

'I d-don't understand,' she murmured eventually.

'Rasmus took it from Rico,' Leo explained. 'You know, Natasha,' he said dryly then, 'you possess more honour than I do. Even when he showed you evidence of my meeting with Gianna in Paris, you still could not take your revenge on me by signing your money over to him.'

She did not want to talk about his betrayal with Gianna. In fact, she began to feel sick just by recalling it. 'I signed for an empty account,' she pointed out.

'But you still signed Natasha *Christakis* instead of Natasha *Moyles*, which meant that Rico could not touch the account, even an empty one.'

'So what are you accusing me of now?' she demanded helplessly.

'Nothing.' Leo sighed.

'So, how did you get Rico to hand this over?' she asked him next.

'Rasmus—persuaded him.'

'Ah, good old Rasmus,' she mocked, recalling the way her minder had had his phone to his ear from the moment that Rico had put in an appearance. It was a shame that Rasmus did not extend his loyalty to her or maybe he would have felt duty-bound to tell her about his employer's night spent in Paris.

And remembering *that* brought Natasha to her feet. 'Does this prison have a bedroom to which I can escape?' she asked stiffly.

'My bedroom,' he confirmed.

'Not this side of hell, Leo,' Natasha informed him coldly. 'I come too expensive even for you from now on.'

'Then name your price....'

Turning on him, Natasha almost threw some obscene figure at him just to see how he would react! But she didn't. In the end she went for blunt honesty. 'A speedy way off this island and an even speedier divorce!' she flicked out, then turned to walk back to the house.

'Deal,' Leo said, bringing her to a taut-shouldered standstill after only two steps. 'For one more night in my bed,' he extended, 'I will arrange your transport away from here.'

'I can't believe even you dared to say that,' she whispered.

'Why not? I am the world's worst cynic who believes everyone has their price. If escape from here and divorce is your price, *agape mou*, then I am willing to pay it—for my own price.'

Natasha walked on, stiff-backed and quivering with offence. Leo followed, feeling suddenly rejuvenated and—more importantly—hungry for the fight. What he had done that afternoon had been pretty much unforgivable. He'd accepted that even before he had watched her take that long walk down his drive. What his beautiful, proud, icy wife had just unwittingly done was to hand him his weapon of salvation and his last chance to put this right between them.

'You just s-stay away from me!' she shrilled when she heard his footsteps closing in on her.

'I'm wildly in love with you—how can I stay away?'

'How *dare* you say that?' Natasha swung around on him,

eyes like glistening blue chips of hurt. 'What do you know about love, Leo? You would not know how to recognise it!'

'And you do?' he threw back. 'You were supposed to be in love with Rico, but where is that broken-hearted love now?'

Pulling in a deep breath, Natasha snapped her lips together. A tense spin of her body and she was continuing up the path and into the house.

Leo followed, more relaxed the more tense that she became. 'You know I'm madly jealous of Rico,' he offered up from the open French windows. 'I have been jealous of him since I first saw you with him. But I refused to recognise what was wrong with me each time I attacked you—'

'With your nasty sarcasms aimed to make me feel small?'

'I wanted you to notice me— What are you looking for?'

'I noticed you, Leo. My purse.'

'On the floor marking the spot where I last kissed you,' he indicated. 'You have to drop the purse, you see, so you can dig your nails into my neck in case I decide to stop.'

Face burning fire now, Natasha went and picked the purse up then walked out of the room.

'Ask yourself, *agape mou*, did you ever see me with another woman from the first night we met?'

She swung around. 'Gianna, in your bedroom, calling me her whoring substitute?' she offered up. 'Gianna, in Paris, coaxing you into a hotel for a cosy—chat?'

Leo sighed. 'I can explain about Gianna. She—'

'Do I look like I *want* an explanation?' Natasha flicked out.

The stairs drew her. She hadn't a clue where she was going, but it suited Leo that she'd taken that direction.

'Middle door on the right,' he offered helpfully. 'My room. My bed. My offer still in place. I will even throw in a candlelit dinner for two on the beach— Damn.'

He should have seen it coming. He had, after all, been

goading her towards some kind of reaction since he'd decided to go on the offensive. But to watch her drop down on one of the stairs and bury her face in her hands, then start weeping, was more than he'd bargained for.

He was up there and squatting in front of her and pulling her into his chest before she had a chance to let out the second sob. 'No,' he roughed out. 'Not the tears, Natasha. You were supposed to fly at me with your fists so I could catch you and kiss you out of your head.'

'I hate you,' she sobbed. 'You're so—'

'Loathsome, I know,' he sighed out. 'I'm sorry.'

'You think I'm a thief.'

'I have never, for one second, believed you were a thief,' he denied. 'I have a split personality. I can go wild with jealousy over Rico and can still recognise that you're the most honest person I know.'

The sobs stopped coming; she replaced them with a forlorn sniff. 'That wasn't what you said when you made me come to Greece with you.'

'I was fighting for my woman. I was prepared to say or do anything.'

'You were *ruthless* this afternoon.'

'Unforgivably so,' he agreed. 'Give me one night in our bed and I will make it up to you.'

'Then let me go tomorrow?'

'Ah.' That was all, just that rueful *Ah*, and Natasha knew she had caught him out.

'And I always believed you spoke only the truth,' she denounced, frowning when she caught the way her fingers were toying with the buttons on his shirt and wondering why she was letting them do that. 'It was your only saving grace as far as I could tell.'

'I thought the fantastic sex was.'

She shook her head, still watching as a section of hair-roughened, bronzed skin appeared close enough for her to kiss. He smelled warm—of Leo, masculine and tempting.

'I need a shower....'

Natasha shook her head as another button gave on the shirt. His hands moved on her back. 'Dangerous, Natasha,' he warned her gently.

Too late. Her tongue snaked out and she licked.

That's it! he might as well have announced as he rose up to his full height, pulling her up with him, then clamping her hard against his body before mounting the rest of the stairs. 'You know what you are,' he bit out at her. 'You are a man-teaser.'

'I am not!' Natasha denied.

'You tell me you hate me then you lick me as if I am the sweetest-tasting thing in your world! If that is not man teasing, then I don't know what is.'

'I am still not going to bed with you!'

'No?' He opened up his arms and dropped her like a discarded bundle on a bed and was right there with her before she could recover from the drop, his fingers already busy with the buttons on her jacket. 'You pull this blue thing on like a suit of armour...' he muttered.

The jacket flew open to reveal a skimpy lilac silk camisole, then he was reaching round beneath her so he could unzip her skirt. 'When I think of the years I indulged in classy, sophisticated sex with classy, sophisticated women—' he gritted.

'I don't want to hear about your other women,' Natasha protested, trying to stop him from undressing her by wriggling her hips.

'Were you listening to anything I have already said?' he husked out. 'There have been no other women since I met you! Before you is none of your business.'

'Then don't *talk* about them!'

'I was trying to make a point—that sex without all of this mad, wild, crazily emotional stuff is rubbish sex! Not that you are ever going to find that out.'

'I might do—after tonight.'

About to remove her skirt altogether, Leo went still. 'So you are staying here with me tonight?'

'I might do,' she repeated coolly. 'I suppose it depends on what you're going to tell me you were doing with Gianna in Paris and if I decide to believe you.'

'Ah.' There it was again, the *Ah* sound that said— Caught me out again, Natasha. And he rolled away from her to stretch out beside her on the bed. 'It was not a hotel in Paris,' he stated flatly. 'It was at a very exclusive private clinic made to look like a hotel, and Rico knew that when he showed you what he did because Gianna has been there countless times before....'

'A clinic that looks like a hotel? Very convenient,' Natasha said dryly. 'Next thing you will be telling me you accidentally bumped into her on the steps.'

'No. I took her there,' Leo sighed out. 'The way she put her nails into you made me decide that it was time for me to get tough. You have to know something about her past to understand Gianna,' he went on heavily. 'Things I did not know about until after we were married and had to find out the hard way,' he admitted. 'She is not a bad person just a— very sad product of a sick upbringing in the centre of a wealthy but corrupt family who taught her that sex equalled love.'

'Oh, that's awful,' Natasha murmured, catching on to what he meant.

'And it is her story, not mine to tell. So let me just say that we had been lovers for a couple of months when she told me she was pregnant. Of course I married her, why not?' He was almost asking himself. 'She was beautiful, great company and about to become the mother of my first child. I saw no problem being faithful to her. Then two weeks after we married I caught her in bed with another man. She tried to tell me it didn't mean anything—but it meant a hell of a lot to me.'

'So you threw her out?'

'Walked out,' he amended. 'A week later she lost the baby and I've never felt so bad or so guilty about anything in my entire life because I had allowed myself to forget the fragile life growing inside her when I walked out. She suffered her first breakdown, which placed her in the Paris clinic for the first time. It was while she was in there that the truth about her past came out. Because I felt sorry for her and she needed someone to care about her, I took her back into my life.'

'Because you loved her,' Natasha murmured.

He turned his head to look at her, dark eyes glowing in the darkening sunset. 'I am not going to lie to you, Natasha, and say she no longer means anything to me,' he stated flatly. 'I did not go into my marriage with her, expecting it to turn out the way that it did. But as for loving her? No, I never did love her the way that you mean. But I did and do still care for her, and, believe me, she really does not have anyone else that does.'

Moving onto her side so she could watch his expression, 'So you—look out for her?' she questioned carefully.

His chiselled jaw tightened. 'I do not sleep with her.'

'That was not what I asked.'

'But you are still thinking it,' he said, reading her face the same as she was reading his. 'I have not slept with Gianna since I took her back into my life. She had another lover within days of arriving back in Athens anyway.' He shrugged. 'The unpalatable fact that she can't help using sex as a substitute for love and affection is not her fault, but I couldn't live with it, though we struggled on for several months before I finally walked out.'

'OK…' It was crazy of her to think that he needed her to touch him, but that was what Natasha sensed in him while he lay there talking himself out. But not yet. 'So you still care for her. You look out for her. You do not sleep with her,' she listed. 'Are you expecting me to accept her as a part of my life, too?'

'Hell, no.' He was suddenly rising up to lean over her and crushing her mouth with a hot kiss. 'That part is over,' he vowed as he drew away again. 'She finally killed my lingering guilt and my sympathy for her when it hit me that it was very fortuitous that Rico happened to catch me with her on the clinic steps.'

Natasha frowned. 'I don't follow—'

'Gianna is good at seducing people to do what she wants them to do—so is Rico, come to that. She wanted you out of my life and he wanted his money. Put the two together, plus the fact that Rico knows what Gianna is like about me, and you have a great conspiracy plot to get you to sign over the money and have you walk out of my life at the same time.'

'Oh, that is so—sick.'

'That's Gianna and Rico,' Leo acknowledged ruefully. 'Now can we talk about you and me? What do *you* want, Natasha?' he questioned her.

Natasha lowered her eyes to look at his mouth. It wasn't smiling. It wasn't even thinking about smiling, his question was that serious.

So what did she want?

She felt his fingers come to rest lightly on her cheekbones, felt the weight of his thighs pressing hers into the bed. She lifted her hands up to his chest and watched her fingertips curl into dark coils of hair and felt, heard—saw him take a slow and careful intake of breath. She saw the wedding band he'd placed on her finger glow as the last of the sun caught hold of it and set the gold on fire.

Then she looked up at him, into his eyes, his dark—dark,

serious eyes. 'You,' she breathed out whisperingly. 'I just want you.'

Vulnerable, Leo saw, so vulnerable her lips had to tremble as she made herself say it as if she was still scared to open up to him with the truth.

He pulled in a deep breath. 'I've changed my mind about this suit,' he said, not looking into her eyes any more. 'I love it. It reminds me of the woman I first fell in love with—'

'M-miss Buttoned Up, you mean?'

'Miss *Sexily* Buttoned Up,' he extended, then pushed himself away from her so he could button her back up again before he rose up off the bed, pulling her up so he could turn her around and do up her skirt zip.

'Why are you doing that?'

'I had forgotten about something.' Transferring his fingers to his shirt buttons, he fastened those, too. Natasha watched as he hid his bronze, muscled body away from her and felt the sting of disappointment.

Then he was taking possession of one of her hands and trailing her out of the bedroom, back down the stairs, back through the living room and back through the French doors, where Natasha pulled to a breathless stop in surprise.

The darkened terrace had been transformed while they'd been upstairs in the bedroom, and was now a flickering wonderland of soft candle-light.

A table had been laid for two and Bernice was just turning away from it. '*Kalispera*.' She smiled at the two of them. 'You ready to eat now?'

Leo answered in his own language, while trailing a silenced Natasha over to the table, then politely held out her chair.

'What's going on?' she managed in bewilderment.

'When I plan something this carefully, I usually follow through with it,' this unusual, hard-crusted, soft-centred man standing there drawled. 'The surprise I promised you,' he explained. 'You had forgotten about it, I see.'

'Oh,' she murmured, because she had forgotten.

Leo smiled as he sat down. 'I was not expecting to do this with us both dressed like this. However…' He reached across the table to take hold of her hands. 'Natasha, this is my home. My real home. The others are just convenient places I use when I need a place to stay. But this island will always be the place I come home to.'

'Well, that's—very nice,' she said, wondering where this was leading.

'More than nice, it's special.' His dark eyes were focused intently on her face. 'I am madly, wildly, jealously in love with you, *agape mou*. I spoiled that part too by telling you so earlier,' he then acknowledged with a rueful tilt to his mouth. 'But I do—love you. If it was not already too late, I would be sitting here now asking you to marry me. Since I've already done that part, too, all I can ask you is, will you live here with me, Natasha? Share my home with me, have my children and bring them up here with me, and make this cynical Greek a very happy man…?'

Natasha didn't know what to say. She hadn't come here expecting him to say any of this. In fact, she'd come here believing that she hated him and that he hated her.

'And this is your surprise?' she asked finally.

His fingers twitched on her fingers because she clearly was not giving him the response he desired. 'Until I tried my best to murder my chances this afternoon.' He nodded. 'Did I murder them?'

The outright challenge from the blunt speaker, Natasha noticed distractedly.

She shook her head.

'Then say something a bit more—positive,' he prompted impatiently, 'because I feel like I am sinking very fast here….'

Sinking fast…she was sinking fast…beneath his spell. 'Yes, please,' she said.

Leo muttered something she didn't catch, then sat back in his seat. 'It must be the suit.' He laughed, though it wasn't a real laugh. 'Would you like to explain to me what the polite *yes, please* covers exactly?'

Now he was cross. Natasha frowned. 'You're sitting there just *expecting* me to say it back to you, aren't you?'

'*Theos,* if you don't love me, then I've caught myself yet another little liar for a wife because every damn thing you do around me *tells* me you love me!'

'All right—I love you!' she announced on a rush of heat. 'I love you,' she repeated. 'But I'm still angry with you, Leo, so words like that don't come easily!'

'Angry about what?' His eyes flickered red with annoyance in the candle-light. 'I've already apologised for—'

'You scared me half to death when you hustled me at the airport!'

'I scared myself more when I thought I wasn't going to catch you before you flew away.'

'Oh,' she said.

'Oh,' he repeated, then climbed back to his feet. 'We are going back to bed.'

He already had hold of her hand again and was pulling her to her feet. 'We can't,' she quavered. 'Bernice—'

'Bernice!' Leo called out as they hit the hallway. 'Hold the dinner. We are going back to bed!'

'God, why do you have to be so openly *blunt?*' Natasha gasped in hot embarrassment.

'OK…you make the nice babies now…' the calm answer came drifting back towards them.

'Even Bernice knows blunt is best.' Leo turned on the stairs to grin down at her.

'All right!' Natasha pulled to a stop, eyes flashing blue flames of anger and brimming defiance. 'So I love you!' she repeated at the top of her voice. 'I don't understand *why* I should love you because, quite *bluntly*, Leo, you drive me up the wall! But—'

He pulled her towards him and kissed her right there on the stairs. Her fingers shot around his neck to stop her tumbling backwards—and because they couldn't help themselves.

'That is why you love me,' he insisted when he eventually pulled back.

'You could be right,' Natasha conceded with her eyes fixed on his oh-so-kissable mouth before she lifted them up to clash with his eyes. 'Do you think we could check it out some more, please…?'

*Demure but defiant...*
*Can three international playboys*
*tame their disobedient brides?*

# Lynne Graham

*presents*

### BRIDES ♥ HUSBANDS

Proud, masculine and passionate, these men are used
to having it all. In stories filled with drama, desire
and secrets of the past, find out how these arrogant
husbands capture their hearts.

## THE GREEK TYCOON'S
## DISOBEDIENT BRIDE
Available December 2008, Book #2779

## THE RUTHLESS MAGNATE'S
## VIRGIN MISTRESS
Available January 2009, Book #2787

## THE SPANISH BILLIONAIRE'S
## PREGNANT WIFE
Available February 2009, Book #2795

# HIRED: FOR THE BOSS'S PLEASURE

She's gone from personal assistant
to mistress—but now he's demanding
she become the boss's bride!

**Read all our fabulous stories this month:**

## MISTRESS: HIRED FOR THE BILLIONAIRE'S PLEASURE
by INDIA GREY

## THE BILLIONAIRE BOSS'S INNOCENT BRIDE
by LINDSAY ARMSTRONG

## HER RUTHLESS ITALIAN BOSS
by CHRISTINA HOLLIS

## MEDITERRANEAN BOSS, CONVENIENT MISTRESS
by KATHRYN ROSS

HPE0209

# HARLEQUIN *Presents*

## *International Billionaires*

### *Life is a game of power and pleasure.*
### *And these men play to win!*

Let Harlequin Presents® take you on a jet-set journey
to meet eight male wonders of the world. From rich
tycoons to royal playboys— they're red-hot and ruthless!

## International Billionaires coming in 2009

**THE PRINCE'S WAITRESS WIFE**
by *Sarah Morgan*, February

**AT THE ARGENTINEAN BILLIONAIRE'S BIDDING**
by *India Grey*, March

**THE FRENCH TYCOON'S PREGNANT MISTRESS**
by *Abby Green*, April

**THE RUTHLESS BILLIONAIRE'S VIRGIN**
by *Susan Stephens*, May

**THE ITALIAN COUNT'S DEFIANT BRIDE**
by *Catherine George*, June

**THE SHEIKH'S LOVE-CHILD**
by *Kate Hewitt*, July

**BLACKMAILED INTO THE GREEK TYCOON'S BED**
by *Carol Marinelli*, August

**THE VIRGIN SECRETARY'S IMPOSSIBLE BOSS**
by *Carol Mortimer*, September

### 8 volumes in all to collect!

**www.eHarlequin.com**

HP12798

# REQUEST YOUR FREE BOOKS!

HARLEQUIN *Presents*

PASSION
GUARANTEED
SEDUCTION

## 2 FREE NOVELS PLUS 2 FREE GIFTS!

**YES!** Please send me 2 FREE Harlequin Presents® novels and my 2 FREE gifts (gifts are worth about $10). After receiving them, if I don't wish to receive any more books, I can return the shipping statement marked "cancel". If I don't cancel, I will receive 6 brand-new novels every month and be billed just $4.05 per book in the U.S. or $4.74 per book in Canada, plus 25¢ shipping and handling per book and applicable taxes, if any*. That's a savings of close to 15% off the cover price! I understand that accepting the 2 free books and gifts places me under no obligation to buy anything. I can always return a shipment and cancel at any time. Even if I never buy another book, the two free books and gifts are mine to keep forever.

106 HDN ERRW  306 HDN ERRL

Name                                    (PLEASE PRINT)

Address                                                           Apt. #

City                          State/Prov.                    Zip/Postal Code

Signature (if under 18, a parent or guardian must sign)

### Mail to the **Harlequin Reader Service:**
**IN U.S.A.:** P.O. Box 1867, Buffalo, NY 14240-1867
**IN CANADA:** P.O. Box 609, Fort Erie, Ontario L2A 5X3

Not valid to current subscribers of Harlequin Presents books.

**Want to try two free books from another line?**
**Call 1-800-873-8635 or visit www.morefreebooks.com.**

* Terms and prices subject to change without notice. N.Y. residents add applicable sales tax. Canadian residents will be charged applicable provincial taxes and GST. Offer not valid in Quebec. This offer is limited to one order per household. All orders subject to approval. Credit or debit balances in a customer's account(s) may be offset by any other outstanding balance owed by or to the customer. Please allow 4 to 6 weeks for delivery. Offer available while quantities last.

**Your Privacy:** Harlequin Books is committed to protecting your privacy. Our Privacy Policy is available online at www.eHarlequin.com or upon request from the Reader Service. From time to time we make our lists of customers available to reputable third parties who may have a product or service of interest to you. If you would prefer we not share your name and address, please check here. ☐

HP08R

I ♥

**HARLEQUIN®** *Presents*

---

BROUGHT TO YOU BY FANS OF
**HARLEQUIN PRESENTS.**

We are its editors and authors
and biggest fans—and we'd
love to hear from YOU!

Subscribe today to our online blog at
**www.iheartpresents.com**

HARLEQUIN *Presents*

kept for his
*Pleasure*

### *She's his mistress on demand!*

Wherever seduction takes place, these fabulously
wealthy, charismatic, sexy men know how to
keep a woman coming back for more!

She's his mistress on demand—but when he
wants her body *and soul* he will be demanding
a whole lot more! Dare we say it…even marriage!

# CONFESSIONS OF A
# MILLIONAIRE'S MISTRESS
## *by Robyn Grady*

**Don't miss any books in
this exciting new miniseries
from Harlequin Presents!**